# Lyre and Lancet: A Story in Scenes by F. Anstey

F. Anstey was the pseudonym of Thomas Anstey Guthrie who was born in Kensington, London on August 8th, 1856, to Augusta Amherst Austen, an organist and composer, and Thomas Anstey Guthrie., a prosperous military tailor

Anstey was educated at King's College School and then at Trinity Hall, Cambridge. Although his education was first rate Anstey could only manage a third-class degree; A Gentlemen's degree as it was euphemistically known.

In 1880 he was called to the bar. However this career path rapidly fell away in his desire to become an author. The successful publication of Vice Versa, in 1882, with the premise of a substitution of a father for his schoolboy son, made his name and reputation as a refreshing and original humorist.

The following year he published a rather more serious work, The Giant's Robe. Interestingly the story is about a plagiarist and Anstey was, ironically, accused of plagiarism in writing the work. Despite good reviews both he and his public knew that his writing career was to be that of a humorist.

In the following years he published prolifically beginning with; The Black Poodle (1884), The Tinted Venus (1885), A Fallen Idol (1886), and Baboo Jabberjee B.A. (1897).

Anstey worked not only as a novelist and short story writer but was also a valued member of the staff at the humorous Punch magazine, in which his voces populi and his parodies of a reciter's stock-piece (Burglar Bill) represent perhaps his best work.

In 1901, his successful farce, The Man from Blankleys, based on a story that originally appeared in Punch, was first produced on stage at the Prince of Wales Theatre, in London.

Anstey had become a writer, and a successful one at that, of many talents.

Many more of his stories were made into plays and films over the years. Others were simply taken for the premise alone, usually with no credit to the original author.

By the end of the First World War Anstey's original publications had slowed to a crawl and he seemed rather more interested in translating and publishing some works of Moliere.

Thomas Anstey Guthrie died of pneumonia on March 10th, 1934 in London.

His self-deprecating autobiography, A Long Retrospect, was published in 1936.

## Index of Contents

CHARACTERS

GALFRID UNDERSHELL (a minor poet)
JAMES SPURRELL, M.R.C.V.S
THE COUNTESS OF CANTIRE
LADY MAISIE MULL (her daughter)
SIR RUPERT CULVERIN
LADY CULVERIN
LADY RHONDA COKAYNE
MRS. BROOKE-CHATTERIS
MISS SPELWANE
THE BISHOP OF BIRCHESTER
LORD LULLINGTON
LADY LULLINGTON
MRS. EARWAKER
THE HONOURABLE BERTIE PILLINER
CAPTAIN THICKNESSE
ARCHIE BEARPARK
MR. SHORTHORN
DRYSDALE (a journalist)
TANRAKE (a job-master)
EMMA PHILLIPSON - (maid to LADY CANTIRE)
MRS POMFRET (housekeeper at Wyvern Court)
MISS STICKLER (maid to LADY CULVERIN)

MISS DOLMAN (maid to LADY RHONDA COKAYNE)
MLLE. CHIFFON (maid to MISS SPELWANE)
M. RIDEVOS (chef at Wyvern)
TREDWELL (butler at Wyvern)
STEPTOE (valet to SIR RUPERT CULVERIN)
THOMAS (a footman)
ADAMS (stud-groom)
CHECKLEY (head coachman)
Steward's Room Boy, etc.

## PART I

SHADOWS CAST BEFORE

In Sir RUPERT CULVERIN'S Study at Wyvern Court. It is a rainy Saturday morning in February. SIR RUPERT is at his writing-table, as LADY CULVERIN enters with a deprecatory air.

LADY CULVERIN - So here you are, Rupert! Not very busy, are you? I won't keep you a moment. (She goes to a window.) Such a nuisance it's turning out wet, with all these people in the house, isn't it?

SIR RUPERT CULVERIN - Well, I was thinking that, as there's nothing doing out of doors, I might get a chance to knock off some of these confounded accounts, but—(resignedly)—if you think I ought to go and look after—

LADY CULVERIN - No, no; the men are playing billiards, and the women are in the morning-room—they're all right. I only wanted to ask you about to-night. You know the Lullingtons, and the dear Bishop and Mrs. Rodney, and one or two other people are coming to dinner? Well, who ought to take in Rohesia?

SIR RUPERT CULVERIN  (in dismay) - Rohesia! No idea she was coming down this week!

LADY CULVERIN - Yes, by the 4.45. With dear Maisie. Surely you knew that?

SIR RUPERT CULVERIN - In a sort of way; didn't realize it was so near, that's all.

LADY CULVERIN - It's some time since we had her last. And she wanted to come. I didn't think you would like me to write and put her off.

SIR RUPERT CULVERIN - Put her off? Of course I shouldn't, Albinia. If my only sister isn't welcome at Wyvern at any time—I say at any time—where the deuce is she welcome?

LADY CULVERIN - I don't know, dear Rupert. But—but about the table?

SIR RUPERT CULVERIN - So long as you don't put her near me—that's all I care about.

LADY CULVERIN - I mean—ought I to send her in with Lord Lullington, or the Bishop?

SIR RUPERT CULVERIN - Why not let 'em toss up? Loser gets her, of course.

LADY CULVERIN - Rupert! As if I could suggest such a thing to the Bishop! I suppose she'd better go in with Lord Lullington—he's Lord Lieutenant—and then it won't matter if she does advocate Disestablishment. Oh, but I forgot; she thinks the House of Lords ought to be abolished too!

SIR RUPERT CULVERIN - Whoever takes Rohesia in is likely to have a time of it. Talked poor Cantire into his tomb a good ten years before he was due there. Always lecturing, and domineering, and laying down the law, as long as I can remember her. Can't stand Rohesia—never could!

LADY CULVERIN - I don't think you ought to say so, really, Rupert. And I'm sure I get on very well with her—generally.

SIR RUPERT CULVERIN - Because you knock under to her.

LADY CULVERIN - I'm sure I don't, Rupert—at least, no more than everybody else. Dear Rohesia is so strong-minded and advanced and all that, she takes such an interest in all the new movements and things, that she can't understand contradiction; she is so democratic in her ideas, don't you know.

SIR RUPERT CULVERIN - Didn't prevent her marrying Cantire. And a democratic Countess—it's downright unnatural!

LADY CULVERIN - She believes it's her duty to set an example and meet the People half-way. That reminds me—did I tell you Mr. Clarion Blair is coming down this evening, too?—only till Monday, Rupert.

SIR RUPERT CULVERIN - Clarion Blair! never heard of him.

LADY CULVERIN - I suppose I forgot. Clarion Blair isn't his real name, though; it's only a—an alias.

SIR RUPERT CULVERIN - Don't see what any fellow wants with an alias. What is his real name?

LADY CULVERIN - Well, I know it was something ending in "ell," but I mislaid his letter. Still, Clarion Blair is the name he writes under; he's a poet, Rupert, and quite celebrated, so I'm told.

SIR RUPERT CULVERIN - (uneasily) A poet! What on earth possessed you to ask a literary fellow down here? Poetry isn't much in our way; and a poet will be, confoundedly!

LADY CULVERIN - I really couldn't help it, Rupert. Rohesia insisted on my having him to meet her. She likes meeting clever and interesting people. And this Mr. Blair, it seems, has just written a volume of verses which are finer than anything that's been done since—well, for ages!

SIR RUPERT CULVERIN - What sort of verses?

LADY CULVERIN - Well, they're charmingly bound. I've got the book in the house, somewhere. Rohesia told me to send for it; but I haven't had time to read it yet.

SIR RUPERT CULVERIN - Shouldn't be surprised if Rohesia hadn't, either.

LADY CULVERIN - At all events, she's heard it talked about. The young man's verses have made quite a sensation; they're so dreadfully clever and revolutionary, and morbid and pessimistic, and all that, so she made me promise to ask him down here to meet her!

SIR RUPERT CULVERIN - Devilish thoughtful of her.

LADY CULVERIN - Wasn't it? She thought it might be a valuable experience for him; he's sprung, I believe, from quite the middle-class.

SIR RUPERT CULVERIN - Don't see myself why he should be sprung on us. Why can't Rohesia ask him to one of her own places?

LADY CULVERIN - I dare say she will, if he turns out to be quite presentable. And, of course, he may, Rupert, for anything we can tell.

SIR RUPERT CULVERIN - Then you've never seen him yourself! How did you manage to ask him here, then?

LADY CULVERIN - Oh, I wrote to him through his publishers. Rohesia says that's the usual way with literary persons one doesn't happen to have met. And he wrote to say he would come.

SIR RUPERT CULVERIN - So we're to have a morbid revolutionary poet staying in the house, are we? He'll come down to dinner in a flannel shirt and no tie—or else a red one—if he don't bring down a beastly bomb and try to blow us all up! You'll find you've made a mistake, Albinia, depend upon it.

LADY CULVERIN - Dear Rupert, aren't you just a little bit narrow? You forget that nowadays the very best houses are proud to entertain Genius—no matter what their opinions and appearance may be. And besides, we don't know what changes may be coming. Surely it is wise and prudent to conciliate the clever young men who might inflame the masses against us. Rohesia thinks so; she says it may be our only chance of stemming the rising tide of Revolution, Rupert!

SIR RUPERT CULVERIN - Oh, if Rohesia thinks a revolution can be stemmed by asking a few poets down from Saturday to Monday, she might do her share of the stemming at all events.

LADY CULVERIN - But you will be nice to him, Rupert, won't you?

SIR RUPERT CULVERIN - I don't know that I'm in the habit of being uncivil to any guest of yours in this house, my dear, but I'll be hanged if I grovel to him, you know; the tide ain't as high as all that. But it's an infernal nuisance, 'pon my word it is; you must look after him yourself. I can't. I don't know what to talk to geniuses about; I've forgotten all the poetry I ever learnt. And if he comes out with any of his Red Republican theories in my hearing, why—

LADY CULVERIN - Oh, but he won't, dear. I'm certain he'll be quite mild and inoffensive. Look at Shakespeare—the bust, I mean—and he began as a poacher!

SIR RUPERT CULVERIN - Ah, and this chap would put down the Game Laws if he could, I dare say; do away with everything that makes the country worth living in. Why, if he had his way, Albinia, there wouldn't be—

LADY CULVERIN - I know, dear, I know. And you must make him see all that from your point. Look, the weather really seems to be clearing a little. We might all of us get out for a drive or something after lunch. I would ride, if Deerfoot's all right again; he's the only horse I ever feel really safe upon, now.

SIR RUPERT CULVERIN - Sorry, my dear, but you'll have to drive then. Adams tells me the horse is as lame as ever this morning, and he don't know what to make of it. He suggested having Horsfall over, but I've no faith in the local vets myself, so I wired to town for old Spavin. He's seen Deerfoot before, and we could put him up for a night or two. (To TREDWELL, the butler, who enters with a telegram.) Eh, for me? just wait, will you, in case there's an answer. (As he opens it.) Ah, this is from Spavin—h'm, nuisance! "Regret unable to leave at present, bronchitis, junior partner could attend immediately if required.— Spavin." Never knew he had a partner.

TREDWELL - I did hear, Sir Rupert, as Mr. Spavin was looking out for one quite recent, being hasthmatical, m'lady, and so I suppose this is him as the telegram alludes to.

SIR RUPERT CULVERIN - Very likely. Well, he's sure to be a competent man. We'd better have him, eh, Albinia?

LADY CULVERIN - Oh yes, and he must stay till Deerfoot's better. I'll speak to Pomfret about having a room ready in the East Wing for him. Tell him to come by the 4.45, Rupert. We shall be sending the omnibus in to meet that.

SIR RUPERT CULVERIN - All right, I've told him. (Giving the form to TREDWELL.) See that that's sent off at once, please. (After TREDWELL has left.) By the way, Albinia, Rohesia may kick up a row if she has to come up in the omnibus with a vet, eh?

LADY CULVERIN - Goodness, so she might! but he needn't go inside. Still, if it goes on raining like this— I'll tell Thomas to order a fly for him at the station, and then there can't be any bother about it.


PART II

SELECT PASSAGES FROM A COMING POET

In the Morning Room at Wyvern. LADY RHONDA COKAYNE, MRS BROOKE-CHATTERIS, and MISS VIVIEN SPELWANE are comfortably established near the fireplace. The HON. BERTIE PILLINER, CAPTAIN THICKNESSE, and ARCHIE BEARPARK, have just drifted in.

MISS SPELWANE - Why, you don't mean to say you've torn yourselves away from your beloved billiards already? Quite wonderful!

BERTIE PILLINER - It's too horrid of you to leave us to play all by ourselves! We've all got so cross and fractious we've come in here to be petted!

[He arranges himself at her feet, so as to exhibit a very neat pair of silk socks and pumps.

CAPTAIN THICKNESSE - (to himself). Do hate to see a fellow come down in the mornin' with evenin' shoes on!

ARCHIE BEARPARK - (to BERTIE PILLINER). You speak for yourself, Pillener. I didn't come to be petted. Came to see if LADY RHONDA wouldn't come and toboggan down the big staircase on a tea-tray. Do! It's clinkin' sport!

CAPTAIN THICKNESSE - (to himself). If there's one thing I can't stand, it's a rowdy bullyraggin' ass like Archie!

LADY RHONDA - Ta muchly, dear boy, but you don't catch me travellin' downstairs on a tea-tray twice—it's just a bit too clinkin', don't you know!

ARCHIE BEARPARK - (disappointed). Why, there's a mat at the bottom of the stairs! Well, if you won't, let's get up a cushion fight, then. Bertie and I will choose sides. Pilliner, I'll toss you for first pick up—come out of that, do.

BERTIE PILLINER - (lazily). Thanks, I'm much too comfy where I am. And I don't see any point in romping and rumpling one's hair just before lunch. Well, you are slack. And there's a good hour still before lunch. Thicknesse, you suggest something, there's a dear old chap.

CAPTAIN THICKNESSE - (after a mental effort). Suppose we all go and have another look round at the gees—eh, what?

BERTIE PILLINER - I beg to oppose. Do let's show some respect for the privacy of the British hunter. Why should I go and smack them on their fat backs, and feel every one of their horrid legs twice in one morning? I shouldn't like a horse coming into my bedroom at all hours to smack me on the back. I should hate it!

MRS. BROOKE-CHATTERIS - I love them—dear things! But still, it's so wet, and it would mean going up and changing our shoes too—perhaps Lady Rhonda—

[LADY RHONDA flatly declines to stir before lunch.

CAPTAIN THICKNESSE - (resentfully). Only thought it was better than loafin' about, that's all. (To himself.) I do bar a woman who's afraid of a little mud. (He saunters up to Miss SPELWANE and absently pulls the ear of a Japanese spaniel on her knee.) Poo' little fellow, then!

MISS SPELWANE - Poor little fellow? On my lap!

CAPTAIN THICKNESSE - Oh, it—ah—didn't occur to me that he was on your lap. He don't seem to mind that.

MISS SPELWANE - No? How forbearing of him! Would you mind not standing quite so much in my light? I can't see my work.

CAPTAIN THICKNESSE - (to himself, retreating). That girl's always fishin' for compliments. I didn't rise that time, though. It's precious slow here. I've a good mind to say I must get back to Aldershot this afternoon.

[He wanders aimlessly about the room; ARCHIE BEARPARK looks out of window with undisguised boredom.

LADY RHONDA - I say, if none of you are goin' to be more amusin' than this, you may as well go back to your billiards again.

BERTIE PILLINER - Dear Lady Rhonda, how cruel of you! You'll have to let me stay. I'll be so good. Look here, I'll read aloud to you. I can—quite prettily. What shall it be? You don't care? No more do I. I'll take the first that comes. (He reaches for the nearest volume on a table close by.) How too delightful! Poetry—which I know you all adore.

[He turns over the leaves.

LADY RHONDA - If you ask me, I simply loathe it.

BERTIE PILLINER - Ah, but then you never heard me read it, you know. Now, here is a choice little bit, stuck right up in a corner, as if it had been misbehaving itself. "Disenchantment" it's called.

[He reads.
"My Love has sicklied unto Loath,
And foul seems all that fair I fancied
The lily's sheen a leprous growth,
The very buttercups are rancid!"

ARCHIE BEARPARK - Jove! The Johnny who wrote that must have been feelin' chippy!

BERTIE PILLINER - He gets cheaper than that in the next poem. This is his idea of "Abasement."

[He reads.
"With matted head a-dabble in the dust,
And eyes tear-sealèd in a saline crust,
I lie all loathly in my rags and rust
Yet learn that strange delight may lurk in self-disgust."

Now, do you know, I rather like that—it's so deliciously decadent!

LADY RHONDA - I should call it utter rot, myself.

BERTIE PILLINER - (blandly) Forgive me, Lady Rhonda. "Utterly rotten," if you like, but not "utter rot." There's a difference, really. Now, I'll read you a quaint little production which has dropped down to the bottom of the page, in low spirits, I suppose. "Stanza written in Depression near Dulwich."

[He reads.

"The lark soars up in the air;
The toad sits tight in his hole;
And I would I were certain which of the pair
Were the truer type of my soul!"

ARCHIE BEARPARK - I should be inclined to back the toad, myself.

MISS SPELWANE - If you must read, do choose something a little less dismal. Aren't there any love songs?

BERTIE PILLINER - I'll look. Yes, any amount—here's one. (He reads.)
"To My Lady."
"Twine, lanken fingers lily-lithe,
Gleam, slanted eyes all beryl-green,
Pout, blood-red lips that burst awrithe,
Then—kiss me, Lady Grisoline!"

MISS SPELWANE - (interested). So that's his type. Does he mention whether she did kiss him?

BERTIE PILLINER - Probably. Poets are always privileged to kiss and tell. I'll see ... h'm, ha, yes; he does mention it ... I think I'll read something else. Here's a classical specimen.

[He reads.
"Uprears the monster now his slobberous head,
Its filamentous chaps her ankles brushing;
Her twice-five roseal toes are cramped in dread,
Each maidly instep mauven-pink is flushing."

And so on, don't you know.... Now I'll read you a regular rouser called "A Trumpet Blast." Sit tight, everybody!

[He reads.
"Pale Patricians, sunk in self-indulgence,
(One for you, dear Archie!)
Blink your blearèd eyes.
(Blink, pretty creatures, blink!) Behold the Sun—
 Burst proclaim, in purpurate effulgence,
Demos dawning, and the Darkness—done!"

[General hilarity, amidst which LADY CULVERIN enters.

LADY CULVERIN - So glad you all contrive to keep your spirits up, in spite of this dismal weather. What is it that's amusing you all so much, eh, dear Vivien?

MISS SPELWANE - Bertie Pilliner has been reading aloud to us, dear Lady Culverin—the most ridiculous poetry—made us all simply shriek. What's the name of it? (Taking the volume out of BERTIE'S hand.) Oh, Andromeda, and other Poems. By Clarion Blair.

LADY CULVERIN - (coldly) Bertie Pilliner can turn everything into ridicule, we all know; but probably you are not aware that these particular poems are considered quite wonderful by all competent judges. Indeed, my sister-in-law—

ALL - (in consternation) Lady Cantire! Is she the author? Oh, of course, if we'd had any idea—

LADY CULVERIN - I've no reason to believe that Lady Cantire ever composed any poetry. I was only going to say that she was most interested in the author, and as she and my niece Maisie are coming to us this evening—

MISS SPELWANE - Dear Lady Culverin, the verses are quite, quite beautiful; it was only the way they were read.

LADY CULVERIN - I am glad to hear you say so, my dear, because I'm also expecting the pleasure of seeing the author here, and you will probably be his neighbour to-night. I hope, Bertie, that you will remember that this young man is a very distinguished genius; there is no wit that I can discover in making fun of what one doesn't happen to understand.

[She passes on.

Bertie (plaintively, after LADY CULVERIN has left the room). May I trouble somebody to scrape me up? I'm pulverised! But really, you know, a real live poet at Wyvern! I say, Miss Spelwane, how will you like to have him dabbling his matted head next to you at dinner, eh?

MISS SPELWANE - Perhaps I shall find a matted head more entertaining than a smooth one. And, if you've quite done with that volume, I should like to have a look at it.

[She retires with it to her room.

ARCHIE BEARPARK - (to himself). I'm not half sorry this Poet-johnny's comin'; I never caught a Bard in a booby-trap yet.

CAPTAIN THICKNESSE - (to himself). She's coming—this very evenin'! And I was nearly sayin' I must get back to Aldershot!

LADY RHONDA - So Lady Cantire's comin'; we shall all have to be on our hind legs now! But Maisie's a dear thing. Do you know her, Captain Thicknesse?

CAPTAIN THICKNESSE - I—I used to meet Lady Maisie Mull pretty often at one time; don't know if she'll remember it, though.

LADY RHONDA - She'll love meetin' this writin' man—she's so fearfully romantic. I heard her say once that she'd give anythin' to be idealized by a great poet—sort of—what's their names—Petrarch and Beatrice business, don't you know. It will be rather amusin' to see whether it comes off—won't it?

CAPTAIN THICKNESSE - (choking). I—ah—no affair of mine, really. (To himself.) I'm not intellectual enough for her, I know that. Suppose I shall have to stand by and look on at the Petrarchin'. Well, there's always Aldershot!

[The luncheon gong sounds, to the general relief and satisfaction.

## PART III

Opposite a Railway Bookstall at a London Terminus.

TIME—Saturday, 4.25 P.M.

DRYSDALE - (to his friend, GALFRID UNDERSHELL, whom he is "seeing off"). Twenty minutes to spare; time enough to lay in any quantity of light literature.

UNDERSHELL - (in a head voice). I fear the merely ephemeral does not appeal to me. But I should like to make a little experiment. (To the BOOKSTALL CLERK.) A—do you happen to have a copy left of Clarion Blair's Andromeda?

CLERK - Not in stock, sir. Never 'eard of the book, but dare say I could get it for you. Here's a Detective Story we're sellin' like 'ot cakes—The Man with the Missing Toe—very cleverly written story, sir.

UNDERSHELL - I merely wished to know—that was all. (Turning with resigned disgust to DRYSDALE.) Just think of it, my dear fellow. At a bookstall like this one feels the pulse, as it were, of Contemporary Culture; and here my Andromeda, which no less an authority than the Daily Chronicle hailed as the uprising of a new and splendid era in English Song-making, a Poetic Renascence, my poor Andromeda, is trampled underfoot by—(choking)—Men with Missing Toes! What a satire on our so-called Progress!

DRYSDALE - That a purblind public should prefer a Shilling Shocker for railway reading when for a modest half-guinea they might obtain a numbered volume of Coming Poetry on hand-made paper! It does seem incredible,—but they do. Well, if they can't read Andromeda on the journey, they can at least peruse a stinger on it in this week's Saturday. Seen it?

UNDERSHELL - No. I don't vex my soul by reading criticisms on my work. I am no Keats. They may howl—but they will not kill me. By the way, the Speaker had a most enthusiastic notice last week.

DRYSDALE - So you saw that then? But you're right not to mind the others. When a fellow's contrived to hang on to the Chariot of Fame, he can't wonder if a few rude and envious beggars call out "Whip behind!" eh? You don't want to get in yet? Suppose we take a turn up to the end of the platform.

[They do.

JAMES SPURRELL, M.R.C.V.S., enters with his friend, THOMAS TANRAKE, of HURDELL AND TANRAKE, Job and Riding Masters, Mayfair.

SPURRELL - Yes, it's lucky for me old Spavin being laid up like this—gives me a regular little outing, do you see? going down to a swell place like this Wyvern Court, and being put up there for a day or two! I shouldn't wonder if they do you very well in the housekeeper's room. (To CLERK.) Give me a Pink Un and last week's Dog Fancier's Guide.

CLERK - We've returned the unsold copies, sir. Could give you this week's; or there's The Rabbit and Poultry Breeder's Journal.

SPURRELL - Oh, rabbits be blowed! (To TANRAKE.) I wanted you to see that notice they put in of Andromeda and me, with my photo and all; it said she was the best bull-bitch they'd seen for many a day, and fully deserved her first prize.

TANRAKE - She's a rare good bitch, and no mistake. But what made you call her such an outlandish name?

SPURRELL - Well, I was going to call her Sal; but a chap at the College thought the other would look more stylish if I ever meant to exhibit her. Andromeda was one of them Roman goddesses, you know.

TANRAKE - Oh, I knew that right enough. Come and have a drink before you start—just for luck—not that you want that.

SPURRELL - I'm lucky enough in most things, Tom; in everything except love. I told you about that girl, you know—Emma—and my being as good as engaged to her, and then, all of a sudden, she went off abroad, and I've never seen or had a line from her since. Can't call that luck, you know. Well, I won't say no to a glass of something.

[They disappear into the refreshment room.

The Countess of CANTIRE enters with her daughter, LADY MAISIE MULL.

LADY CANTIRE - (to FOOTMAN). Get a compartment for us, and two foot-warmers, and a second-class as near ours as you can for Phillipson; then come back here. Stay, I'd better give you Phillipson's ticket. (The Footman disappears in the crowd.) Now we must get something to read on the journey. (To CLERK.) I want a book of some sort—no rubbish, mind; something serious and improving, and not a work of fiction.

CLERK - Exactly so, ma'am. Let me see. Ah, here's Alone with the 'Airy Ainoo. How would you like that?

LADY CANTIRE - (with decision). I should not like it at all.

CLERK - I quite understand. Well, I can give you Three 'Undred Ways of Dressing the Cold Mutton—useful little book for a family, redooced to one and ninepence.

LADY CANTIRE - Thank you. I think I will wait till I am reduced to one and ninepence.

CLERK - Precisely. What do you say to Seven 'Undred Side-splitters for Sixpence? 'Ighly yumerous, I assure you.

LADY CANTIRE - Are these times to split our sides, with so many serious social problems pressing for solution? You are presumably not without intelligence; do you never reflect upon the responsibility you incur in assisting to circulate trivial and frivolous trash of this sort?

CLERK - (dubiously) Well, I can't say as I do, particular, ma'am. I'm paid to sell the books—I don't select 'em.

LADY CANTIRE - That is no excuse for you—you ought to exercise some discrimination on your own account, instead of pressing people to buy what can do them no possible good. You can give me a Society Snippets.

LADY MAISIE - Mamma! A penny paper that says such rude things about the Royal Family!

LADY CANTIRE - It's always instructive to know what these creatures are saying about one, my dear, and it's astonishing how they manage to find out the things they do. Ah, here's Gravener coming back. He's got us a carriage, and we'd better get in.

[She and her daughter enter a first-class compartment; UNDERSHELL and DRYSDALE return.

DRYSDALE - (to UNDERSHELL). Well, I don't see now where the insolence comes in. These people have invited you to stay with them—

UNDERSHELL - But why? Not because they appreciate my work—which they probably only half understand—but out of mere idle curiosity to see what manner of strange beast a Poet may be! And I don't know this Lady Culverin—never met her in my life! What the deuce does she mean by sending me an invitation? Why should these smart women suppose that they are entitled to send for a Man of Genius, as if he was their lackey? Answer me that!

DRYSDALE - Perhaps the delusion is encouraged by the fact that Genius occasionally condescends to answer the bell.

UNDERSHELL - (reddening). Do you imagine I am going down to this place simply to please them?

DRYSDALE - I should think it a doubtful kindness, in your present frame of mind; and, as you are hardly going to please yourself, wouldn't it be more dignified, on the whole, not to go at all?

UNDERSHELL - You never did understand me! Sometimes I think I was born to be misunderstood! But you might do me the justice to believe that I am not going from merely snobbish motives. May I not feel that such a recognition as this is a tribute less to my poor self than to Literature, and that, as such, I have scarcely the right to decline it?

DRYSDALE - Ah, if you put it in that way, I am silenced, of course.

UNDERSHELL - Or what if I am going to show these Patricians that—Poet of the People as I am—they can neither patronise nor cajole me?

DRYSDALE - Exactly, old chap—what if you are?

UNDERSHELL - I don't say that I may not have another reason—a—a rather romantic one—but you would only sneer if I told you! I know you think me a poor creature whose head has been turned by an undeserved success.

DRYSDALE - You're not going to try to pick a quarrel with an old chum, are you? Come, you know well enough I don't think anything of the sort. I've always said you had the right stuff in you, and would show it some day; there are even signs of it in Andromeda here and there; but you'll do better things than that, if you'll only let some of the wind out of your head. I take an interest in you, old fellow, and that's just why it riles me to see you taking yourself so devilish seriously on the strength of a little volume of verse which—between you and me—has been "boomed" for all it's worth, and considerably more. You've only got your immortality on a short repairing lease at present, old boy!

UNDERSHELL - (with bitterness) I am fortunate in possessing such a candid friend. But I mustn't keep you here any longer.

DRYSDALE - Very well. I suppose you're going first? Consider the feelings of the Culverin footman at the other end!

UNDERSHELL - (as he fingers a first-class ticket in his pocket) You have a very low view of human nature! (Here he becomes aware of a remarkably pretty face at a second-class window close by). As it happens, I am travelling second.

[He gets in.

DRYSDALE – (at the window) Well, good-bye, old chap. Good luck to you at Wyvern, and remember—wear your livery with as good a grace as possible.

UNDERSHELL - I do not intend to wear any livery whatever.

[The owner of the pretty face regards UNDERSHELL with interest.

SPURRELL - (coming out of the refreshment room) What, second—with all my exes. paid? Not likely! I'm going to travel in style this journey. No—not a smoker; don't want to create a bad impression, you know. This will do for me.

[He gets into a compartment occupied by Lady CANTIRE and her daughter.

TANRAKE - (at the window) There—you're off now. Pleasant journey to you, old man. Hope you'll enjoy yourself at this Wyvern Court you're going to—and, I say, don't forget to send me that notice of Andromeda when you get back!

[The COUNTESS and LADY MAISIE start slightly; the train moves out of the station.


PART IV

RUSHING TO CONCLUSIONS

In a First-class Compartment.

SPURRELL - (to himself) Formidable old party opposite me in the furs! Nice-looking girl over in the corner; not a patch on my Emma, though! Wonder why I catch 'em sampling me over their papers whenever I look up! Can't be anything wrong with my turn out. Why, of course, they heard Tom talk about my going down to Wyvern Court; think I'm a visitor there and no end of a duke! Well, what snobs some people are, to be sure!

LADY CANTIRE - (to herself) So this is the young poet I made Albinia ask to meet me. I can't be mistaken, I distinctly heard his friend mention Andromeda. H'm, well, it's a comfort to find he's clean! Have I read his poetry or not? I know I had the book, because I distinctly remember telling Maisie she wasn't to read it—but—well, that's of no consequence. He looks clever and quite respectable—not in the least picturesque—which is fortunate. I was beginning to doubt whether it was quite prudent to bring Maisie; but I needn't have worried myself.

LADY MAISIE - (to herself). Here, actually in the same carriage! Does he guess who I am? Somehow—Well, he certainly is different from what I expected. I thought he would show more signs of having thought and suffered; for he must have suffered to write as he does. If mamma knew I had read his poems; that I had actually written to beg him not to refuse Aunt Albinia's invitation! He never wrote back. Of course I didn't put any address; but still, he could have found out from the Red Book if he'd cared. I'm rather glad now he didn't care.

SPURRELL - (to himself). Old girl seems as if she meant to be sociable; better give her an opening. (Aloud.) Hem! would you like the window down an inch or two?

LADY CANTIRE - Not on my account, thank you.

SPURRELL - (to himself). Broke the ice, anyway. (Aloud.) Oh, I don't want it down, but some people have such a mania for fresh air.

LADY CANTIRE - (with a dignified little shiver). Have they? With a temperature as glacial as it is in here! They must be maniacs indeed!

SPURRELL - Well, it is chilly; been raw all day. (To himself.) She don't answer. I haven't broken the ice.

[He produces a memorandum book.

LADY MAISIE - (to herself). He hasn't said anything very original yet. So nice of him not to pose! Oh, he's got a note-book; he's going to compose a poem. How interesting!

SPURRELL - (to himself). Yes, I'm all right if Heliograph wins the Lincolnshire Handicap; lucky to get on at the price I did. Wonder what's the latest about the City and Suburban? Let's see whether the Pink Un has anything about it.

[He refers to the Sporting Times.

LADY MAISIE - (to herself) The inspiration's stopped—what a pity! How odd of him to read the Globe! I thought he was a Democrat!

LADY CANTIRE - Maisie, there's quite a clever little notice in Society Snippets about the dance at Skympings last week. I'm sure I wonder how they pick up these things; it quite bears out what I was told; says the supper arrangements were "simply disgraceful; not nearly enough champagne; and what there was, undrinkable!" So like poor dear Lady Chesepare; never does do things like anybody else. I'm sure I've given her hints enough!

SPURRELL - (to himself, with a suppressed grin). Wants to let me see she knows some swells. Now ain't that paltry?

LADY CANTIRE - (tendering the paper). Would you like to see it, Maisie? Just this bit here; where my finger is.

LADY MAISIE - (to herself, flushing). I saw him smile. What must he think of us, with his splendid scorn for rank? (Aloud.) No, thank you, mamma: such a wretched light to read by!

SPURRELL - (to himself). Chance for me to cut in! (Aloud.) Beastly light, isn't it? 'Pon my word, the company ought to provide us with a dog and string apiece when we get out!

LADY CANTIRE - (bringing a pair of long-handled glasses to bear upon him). I happen to hold shares in this line. May I ask why you consider a provision of dogs and string at all the stations a necessary or desirable expenditure?

SPURRELL - Oh—er—well, you know, I only meant, bring on blindness and that. Harmless attempt at a joke, that's all.

LADY CANTIRE - I see. I scarcely expected that you would condescend to such weakness. I—ah—think you are going down to stay at Wyvern for a few days, are you not?

SPURRELL - (to himself). I was right. What Tom said did fetch the old girl; no harm in humouring her a bit. (Aloud.) Yes—oh yes, they—aw—wanted me to run down when I could.

LADY CANTIRE - I heard they were expecting you. You will find Wyvern a pleasant house—for a short visit.

SPURRELL - (to himself). She heard! Oh, she wants to kid me she knows the Culverins. Rats! (Aloud.) Shall I, though? I dare say.

LADY CANTIRE - Lady Culverin is a very sweet woman; a little limited, perhaps, not intellectual, or quite what one would call the grande dame; but perhaps that could scarcely be expected.

SPURRELL - (vaguely) Oh, of course not—no. (To himself.) If she bluffs, so can I! (Aloud.) It's funny your turning out to be an acquaintance of Lady C.'s, though.

LADY CANTIRE - You think so? But I should hardly call myself an acquaintance.

SPURRELL - (to himself) Old cat's trying to back out of it now; she shan't, though! (Aloud.) Oh, then I suppose you know Sir Rupert best?

LADY CANTIRE - Yes, I certainly know Sir Rupert better.

SPURRELL - (to himself) Oh, you do, do you? We'll see. (Aloud.) Nice cheery old chap, Sir Rupert, isn't he? I must tell him I travelled down in the same carriage with a particular friend of his. (To himself.) That'll make her sit up!

LADY CANTIRE - Oh, then you and my brother Rupert have met already?

SPURRELL - (aghast) Your brother! Sir Rupert Culverin your—! Excuse me—if I'd only known, I—I do assure you I never should have dreamt of saying—!

LADY CANTIRE - (graciously) You've said nothing whatever to distress yourself about. You couldn't possibly be expected to know who I was. Perhaps I had better tell you at once that I am Lady Cantire, and this is my daughter, Lady Maisie Mull. (SPURRELL returns Lady MAISIE'S little bow in the deepest confusion.) We are going down to Wyvern too, so I hope we shall very soon become better acquainted.

SPURRELL - (to himself, overwhelmed). The deuce we shall! I have got myself into a hole this time; I wish I could see my way well out of it! Why on earth couldn't I hold my confounded tongue? I shall look an ass when I tell 'em.

[He sits staring at them in silent embarrassment.

In a Second-class Compartment.

UNDERSHELL - (to himself). Singularly attractive face this girl has; so piquant and so refined! I can't help fancying she is studying me under her eyelashes. She has remarkably bright eyes. Can she be interested in me? Does she expect me to talk to her? There are only she and I—but no, just now I would rather be alone with my thoughts. This Maisie Mull whom I shall meet so soon; what is she like, I wonder? I presume she is unmarried. If I may judge from her artless little letter, she is young and enthusiastic, and she is a passionate admirer of my verse; she is longing to meet me. I suppose some men's vanity would be flattered by a tribute like that. I think I must have none; for it leaves me strangely cold. I did not even reply; it struck me that it would be difficult to do so with any dignity, and she didn't tell me where to write to.... After all, how do I know that this will not end—like everything else—in disillusion? Will not such crude girlish adoration pall upon me in time? If she were exceptionally lovely; or say, even as charming as this fair fellow-passenger of mine—why then, to be sure—but no, something warns me that that is not to be. I shall find her plain, sandy, freckled; she will render me ridiculous by her undiscriminating gush.... Yes, I feel my heart sink more and more at the prospect of this visit. Ah me!

[He sighs heavily.

His Fellow Passenger (to herself). It's too silly to be sitting here like a pair of images, considering that—(Aloud.) I hope you aren't feeling unwell?

UNDERSHELL - Thank you, no, not unwell. I was merely thinking.

HIS FELLOW PASSENGER - You don't seem very cheerful over it, I must say. I've no wish to be inquisitive, but perhaps you're feeling a little low-spirited about the place you're going to?

UNDERSHELL - I—I must confess I am rather dreading the prospect. How wonderful that you should have guessed it!

HIS FELLOW PASSENGER - Oh, I've been through it myself. I'm just the same when I go down to a new place; feel a sort of sinking, you know, as if the people were sure to be disagreeable, and I should never get on with them.

UNDERSHELL - Exactly my own sensations! If I could only be sure of finding one kindred spirit, one soul who would help and understand me. But I daren't let myself hope even for that!

HIS FELLOW PASSENGER - Well, I wouldn't judge beforehand. The chances are there'll be somebody you can take to.

UNDERSHELL - (to himself). What sympathy! What bright, cheerful common sense! (Aloud.) Do you know, you encourage me more than you can possibly imagine!

HIS FELLOW PASSENGER - (retreating). Oh, if you are going to take my remarks like that, I shall be afraid to go on talking to you!

UNDERSHELL - (with pathos). Don't—don't be afraid to talk to me! If you only knew the comfort you give! I have found life very sad, very solitary. And true sympathy is so rare, so refreshing. I—I fear such an appeal from a stranger may seem a little startling; it is true that hitherto we have only exchanged a very few sentences; and yet already I feel that we have something—much—in common. You can't be so cruel as to let all intimacy cease here—it is quite tantalising enough that it must end so soon. A very few more minutes, and this brief episode will be only a memory; I shall have left the little green oasis far behind me, and be facing the dreary desert once more—alone!

HIS FELLOW PASSENGER - (laughing). Well, of all the uncomplimentary things! As it happens, though, "the little green oasis"—as you're kind enough to call me—won't be left behind; not if it's aware of it! I think I heard your friend mention Wyvern Court! Well, that's where I'm going.

UNDERSHELL - (excitedly). You—you are going to Wyvern Court! Why, then, you must be—

[He checks himself.

HIS FELLOW PASSENGER - What were you going to say; what must I be?

UNDERSHELL - (to himself). There is no doubt about it; bright, independent girl; gloves a trifle worn; travels second-class for economy; it must be Miss Mull herself; her letter mentioned Lady Culverin as her aunt. A poor relation, probably. She doesn't suspect that I am— I won't reveal myself just yet; better let it dawn upon her gradually. (Aloud.) Why, I was only about to say, why then you must be going to the same house as I am. How extremely fortunate a coincidence!

HIS FELLOW PASSENGER - That remains to be seen. (To herself.) What a funny little man; such a flowery way of talking for a footman. Oh, but I forgot; he said he wasn't going to wear livery. Well, he would look a sight in it!

## PART V

In a First-class Compartment.

LADY MAISIE - (to herself). Poets don't seem to have much self-possession. He seems perfectly overcome by hearing my name like that. If only he doesn't lose his head completely and say something about my wretched letter!

SPURRELL - (to himself) I'd better tell 'em before they find out for themselves. (Aloud; desperately.) My lady, I—I feel I ought to explain at once how I come to be going down to Wyvern like this.

[LADY MAISIE only just suppresses a terrified protest.

LADY CANTIRE - (benignly amused). My good sir, there's not the slightest necessity; I am perfectly aware of who you are, and everything about you!

SPURRELL - (incredulously). But really I don't see how your ladyship— Why, I haven't said a word that—

LADY CANTIRE - (with a solemn waggishness.) Celebrities who mean to preserve their incognito shouldn't allow their friends to see them off. I happened to hear a certain Andromeda mentioned, and that was quite enough for Me!

SPURRELL - (to himself, relieved). She knows; seen the sketch of me in the Dog Fancier, I expect; goes in for breeding bulls herself, very likely. Well, that's a load off my mind! (Aloud.) You don't say so, my lady. I'd no idea your ladyship would have any taste that way; most agreeable surprise to me, I can assure you!

LADY CANTIRE - I see no reason for surprise in the matter. I have always endeavoured to cultivate my taste in all directions; to keep in touch with every modern development. I make it a rule to read and see everything. Of course, I have no time to give more than a rapid glance at most things; but I hope some day to be able to have another look at your Andromeda. I hear the most glowing accounts from all the judges.

SPURRELL - (to himself). She knows all the judges! She must be in the fancy! (Aloud.) Any time your ladyship likes to name I shall be proud and happy to bring her round for your inspection.

LADY CANTIRE - (with condescension). If you are kind enough to offer me a copy of Andromeda, I shall be most pleased to possess one.

SPURRELL - (to himself). Sharp old customer, this; trying to rush me for a pup. I never offered her one! (Aloud.) Well, as to that, my lady, I've promised so many already, that really I don't—but there—I'll see what I can do for you. I'll make a note of it; you mustn't mind having to wait a bit.

LADY CANTIRE - (raising her eyebrows). I will make an effort to support existence in the meantime.

LADY MAISIE - (to herself). I couldn't have believed that the man who could write such lovely verses should be so—well, not exactly a gentleman! How petty of me to have such thoughts. Perhaps geniuses never are. And as if it mattered! And I'm sure he's very natural and simple, and I shall like him when I know him better.

[The train slackens.

LADY CANTIRE - What station is this? Oh, it is Shuntingbridge. (To SPURRELL, as they get out.) Now, if you'll kindly take charge of these bags, and go and see whether there's anything from Wyvern to meet us—you will find us here when you come back.

On the Platform at Shuntingbridge.

LADY CANTIRE - Ah, there you are, Phillipson! Yes, you can take the jewel-case; and now you had better go and see after the trunks. (PHILLIPSON hurries back to the luggage-van; SPURRELL returns.) Well, Mr.—I always forget names, so I shall call you "Andromeda"—have you found out— The omnibus, is it? Very well, take us to it, and we'll get in.

[They go outside.

UNDERSHELL - (at another part of the platform—to himself). Where has Miss Mull disappeared to? Oh, there she is, pointing out her luggage. What a quantity she travels with! Can't be such a very poor relation. How graceful and collected she is, and how she orders the porters about! I really believe I shall enjoy this visit. (To a PORTER.) That's mine—the brown one with a white star. I want it to go to Wyvern Court—Sir Rupert Culverin's.

PORTER - (shouldering it). Right, sir. Follow me, if you please.

[He disappears with it.

UNDERSHELL - (to himself). I mustn't leave Miss Mull alone. (Advancing to her.) Can I be of any assistance?

PHILLIPSON - It's all done now. But you might try and find out how we're to get to the Court.

[UNDERSHELL departs; is requested to produce his ticket, and spends several minutes in searching every pocket but the right one.

In the Station Yard at Shuntingbridge.

LADY CANTIRE - (from the interior of the Wyvern omnibus, testily, to FOOTMAN). What are we waiting for now? Is my maid coming with us—or how?

FOOTMAN - There's a fly ordered to take her, my lady.

LADY CANTIRE - (to SPURRELL, who is standing below). Then it's you who are keeping us!

SPURRELL - If your ladyship will excuse me. I'll just go and see if they've put out my bag.

LADY CANTIRE - (impatiently). Never mind about your bag. (To FOOTMAN) What have you done with this gentleman's luggage?

FOOTMAN - Everything for the Court is on top now, my lady.

[He opens the door for SPURRELL.

LADY CANTIRE - (to SPURRELL, who is still irresolute). For goodness' sake don't hop about on that step! Come in, and let us start.

LADY MAISIE - Please get in—there's plenty of room!

SPURRELL - (to himself). They are chummy, and no mistake! (Aloud, as he gets in.) I do hope it won't be considered any intrusion—my coming up along with your ladyships, I mean!

LADY CANTIRE - (snappishly). Intrusion! I never heard such nonsense! Did you expect to be asked to run behind? You really mustn't be so ridiculously modest. As if your Andromeda hadn't procured you the entrée everywhere!

[The omnibus starts.

SPURRELL - (to himself). Good old Drummy! No idea I was such a swell. I'll keep my tail up. Shyness ain't one of my failings. (Aloud, to an indistinct mass at the further end of the omnibus, which is unlighted.) Er—hum—pitch dark night, my lady, don't get much idea of the country! (The mass makes no response.) I was saying, my lady, it's too dark to— (The mass snores peacefully.) Her ladyship seems to be taking a snooze on the quiet, my lady. (To LADY MAISIE.) (To himself.) Not that that's the term for it!

LADY MAISIE - (distantly). My mother gets tired rather easily. (To herself.) It's really too dreadful; he makes me hot all over! If he's going to do this kind of thing at Wyvern! And I'm more or less responsible for him, too! I must see if I can't— It will be only kind. (Aloud, nervously.) Mr.—Mr. Blair!

SPURRELL - Excuse me, my lady, not Blair—Spurrell.

LADY MAISIE - Of course, how stupid of me. I knew it wasn't really your name. Mr. Spurrell, then, you—you won't mind if I give you just one little hint, will you?

SPURRELL - I shall take it kindly of your ladyship, whatever it is.

LADY MAISIE - (more nervously still) It's really such a trifle, but—but, in speaking to mamma or me, it isn't at all necessary to say "my lady" or "your ladyship." I—I mean, it sounds rather, well—formal, don't you know!

SPURRELL - (to himself) She's going to be chummy now! (Aloud.) I thought, on a first acquaintance, it was only manners.

LADY MAISIE - Oh—manners? yes, I—I dare say—but still—but still—not at Wyvern, don't you know. If you like, you can call mamma "Lady Cantire," and me "Lady Maisie," now and then, and, of course, my aunt will be "Lady Culverin," but—but if there are other people staying in the house, you needn't call them anything, do you see?

SPURRELL - (to himself). I'm not likely to have the chance! (Aloud.) Well, if you're sure they won't mind it, because I'm not used to this sort of thing, so I put myself entirely in your hands,—for, of course, you know what brought me down here?

LADY MAISIE - (to herself). He means my foolish letter! Oh, I must put a stop to that at once! (In a hurried undertone.) Yes—yes; I—I think I do I mean, I do know—but—but please forget it—indeed, you must!

SPURRELL - (to himself). Forget I've come down as a vet? The Culverins will take care I don't forget that! (Aloud.) But, I say, it's all very well; but how can I? Why, look here; I was told I was to come down here on purpose to—

LADY MAISIE - (on thorns). I know—you needn't tell me! And don't speak so loud! Mamma might hear!

SPURRELL - (puzzled). What if she did? Why, I thought her la—your mother knew!

LADY MAISIE - (to herself). He actually thinks I should tell mamma! Oh, how dense he is! (Aloud.) Yes—yes—of course she knows—but—but you might wake her! And—and please don't allude to it again—to me or—or any one. (To herself.) That I should have to beg him to be silent like this! But what can I do? Goodness only knows what he mightn't say, if I don't warn him!

SPURRELL - (nettled). I don't mind who knows. I'm not ashamed of it, Lady Maisie—whatever you may be!

LADY MAISIE - (to herself, exasperated). He dares to imply that I've done something to be ashamed of! (Aloud, haughtily.) I'm not ashamed—why should I be? Only—oh, can't you really understand that—that one may do things which one wouldn't care to be reminded of publicly? I don't wish it—isn't that enough?

SPURRELL - (to himself). I see what she's at now—doesn't want it to come out that she's travelled down here with a vet! (Aloud, stiffly.) A lady's wish is enough for me at any time. If you're sorry for having gone out of your way to be friendly, why, I'm not the person to take advantage of it. I hope I know how to behave.

[He takes refuge in offended silence.

LADY MAISIE - (to herself). Why did I say anything at all! I've only made things worse—I've let him see that he has an advantage. And he's certain to use it sooner or later—unless I am civil to him. I've offended him now—and I shall have to make it up with him!

SPURRELL - (to himself). I thought all along she didn't seem as chummy as her mother—but to turn round on me like this!

LADY CANTIRE - (waking up). Well, Mr. Andromeda, I should have thought you and my daughter might have found some subject in common; but I haven't heard a word from either of you since we left the station.

LADY MAISIE - (to herself). That's some comfort! (Aloud.) You must have had a nap, mamma. We—we have been talking.

SPURRELL - Oh yes, we have been talking, I can assure you, Lady Cantire!

LADY CANTIRE - Dear me. Well, Maisie, I hope the conversation was entertaining?

LADY MAISIE - M—most entertaining, mamma!

LADY CANTIRE - I'm quite sorry I missed it. (The omnibus stops.) Wyvern at last! But what a journey it's been, to be sure!

SPURRELL - (to himself). I should just think it had. I've never been so taken up and put down in all my life! But it's over now; and, thank goodness, I'm not likely to see any more of 'em!

[He gets out with alacrity.


PART VI

ROUND PEGS IN SQUARE HOLES

In the Entrance Hall at Wyvern.

TREDWELL - (to LADY CANTIRE). This way, if you please, my lady. Her ladyship is in the Hamber Boudwore.

LADY CANTIRE - Wait. (She looks round.) What has become of that young Mr. Androm—? (Perceiving SPURRELL, who has been modestly endeavouring to efface himself.) Ah, there he is! Now, come along, and be presented to my sister-in-law. She'll be enchanted to know you!

SPURRELL - But indeed, my lady, I—I think I'd better wait till she sends for me.

LADY CANTIRE - Wait? Fiddlesticks! What! A famous young man like you! Remember Andromeda, and don't make yourself so ridiculous!

SPURRELL - (miserably). Well, Lady Cantire, if her ladyship says anything, I hope you'll bear me out that it wasn't—

LADY CANTIRE - Bear you out? My good young man, you seem to need somebody to bear you in! Come, you are under my wing. I answer for your welcome—so do as you're told.

SPURRELL - (to himself, as he follows resignedly). It's my belief there'll be a jolly row when I do go in; but it's not my fault!

TREDWELL - (opening the door of the Amber Boudoir). Lady Cantire and Lady Maisie Mull (To SPURRELL.) What name, if you please, sir?

SPURRELL - (dolefully). You can say "James Spurrell"—you needn't bellow it, you know!

TREDWELL - (ignoring this suggestion). Mr. James Spurrell.

SPURRELL - (to himself, on the threshold). If I don't get the chuck for this, I shall be surprised, that's all!

[He enters.

In a Fly.

UNDERSHELL - (to himself). Alone with a lovely girl, who has no suspicion, as yet, that I am the poet whose songs have thrilled her with admiration! Could any situation be more romantic? I think I must keep up this little mystification as long as possible.

PHILLIPSON - (to herself). I wonder who he is? Somebody's Man, I suppose. I do believe he's struck with me. Well, I've no objection. I don't see why I shouldn't forget Jim now and then—he's quite forgotten me! (Aloud.) They might have sent a decent carriage for us instead of this ramshackle old summerhouse. We shall be hours getting to the house at this rate!

UNDERSHELL - (gallantly). For my part, I care not how long we may be. I feel so unspeakably content to be where I am.

PHILLIPSON - (disdainfully). In this mouldy, lumbering old concern? You must be rather easily contented, then!

UNDERSHELL - (dreamily). It travels only too swiftly. To me it is a veritable enchanted car, drawn by a magic steed.

PHILLIPSON - I don't know whether he's magic—but I'm sure he's lame. And stuffiness is not my notion of enchantment.

UNDERSHELL - I'm not prepared to deny the stuffiness. But cannot you guess what has transformed this vehicle for me—in spite of its undeniable shortcomings—or must I speak more plainly still?

PHILLIPSON - Well, considering the shortness of our acquaintance, I must say you've spoken quite plainly enough as it is!

UNDERSHELL - I know I must seem unduly expansive, and wanting in reserve; and yet that is not my true disposition. In general, I feel an almost fastidious shrinking from strangers—

PHILLIPSON - (with a little laugh). Really? I shouldn't have thought it!

UNDERSHELL - Because, in the present case, I do not—I cannot—feel as if we were strangers. Some mysterious instinct led me, almost from the first, to associate you with a certain Miss Maisie Mull.

PHILLIPSON - Well, I wonder how you discovered that. Though you shouldn't have said "Miss"—Lady Maisie Mull is the proper form.

UNDERSHELL - (to himself). Lady Maisie Mull! I attach no meaning to titles—and yet nothing but rank could confer such perfect ease and distinction. (Aloud.) I should have said Lady Maisie Mull, undoubtedly—forgive my ignorance. But at least I have divined you. Does nothing tell you who and what I may be?

PHILLIPSON - Oh, I think I can give a tolerable guess at what you are.

UNDERSHELL - You recognize the stamp of the Muse upon me, then?

PHILLIPSON - Well, I shouldn't have taken you for a groom exactly.

UNDERSHELL - (with some chagrin). You are really too flattering!

PHILLIPSON - Am I? Then it's your turn now. You might say you'd never have taken me for a lady's maid!

UNDERSHELL - I might—if I had any desire to make an unnecessary and insulting remark.

PHILLIPSON - Insulting? Why, it's what I am! I'm maid to LADY MAISIE - I thought your mysterious instinct told you all about it?

UNDERSHELL - (to himself—after the first shock). A lady's maid! Gracious Heaven! What have I been saying—or rather, what haven't I? (Aloud.) To—to be sure it did. Of course, I quite understand that. (To himself.) Oh, confound it all, I wish we were at Wyvern!

PHILLIPSON - And, after all, you've never told me who you are. Who are you?

UNDERSHELL - (to himself). I must not humiliate this poor girl! (Aloud.) I? Oh—a very insignificant person, I assure you! (To himself.) This is an occasion in which deception is pardonable—even justifiable!

PHILLIPSON - Oh, I knew that much. But you let out just now you had to do with a Mews. You aren't a rough-rider, are you?

UNDERSHELL - N—not exactly—not a rough-rider. (To himself.) Never on a horse in my life!—unless I count my Pegasus. (Aloud.) But you are right in supposing I am connected with a muse—in one sense.

PHILLIPSON - I said so, didn't I? Don't you think it was rather clever of me to spot you, when you're not a bit horsey-looking?

UNDERSHELL - (with elaborate irony). Accept my compliments on a power of penetration which is simply phenomenal!

PHILLIPSON - (giving him a little push). Oh, go along—it's all talk with you—I don't believe you mean a word you say!

UNDERSHELL - (to himself). She's becoming absolutely vulgar. (Aloud.) I don't—I don't; it's a manner I have; you mustn't attach any importance to it—none whatever!

PHILLIPSON - What! Not to all those high-flown compliments? Do you mean to tell me you are only a gay deceiver, then?

UNDERSHELL - (in horror). Not a deceiver, no; and decidedly not gay. I mean I did mean the compliments, of course. (To himself.) I mustn't let her suspect anything, or she'll get talking about it; it would be too horrible if this were to get round to Lady Maisie or the Culverins—so undignified; and it would ruin all my prestige! I've only to go on playing a part for a few minutes, and—maid or not—she's a most engaging girl!

[He goes on playing the part, with the unexpected result of sending Miss PHILLIPSON into fits of uncontrollable laughter.

At a Back Entrance at Wyvern. The Fly has just set down PHILLIPSON and UNDERSHELL.

TREDWELL - (receiving PHILLIPSON). Lady Maisie's maid, I presume? I'm the butler here—Mr. TREDWELL - Your ladies arrived some time back. I'll take you to the housekeeper, who'll show you their rooms, and where yours is, and I hope you'll find everything comfortable. (In an undertone, indicating UNDERSHELL, who is awaiting recognition in the doorway.) Do you happen to know who it is with you?

PHILLIPSON - (in a whisper). I can't quite make him out—he's so flighty in his talk. But he says he belongs to some Mews or other.

TREDWELL - Oh, then I know who he is. We expect him right enough. He's a partner in a crack firm of Vets. We've sent for him special. I'd better see to him, if you don't mind finding your own way to the housekeeper's room, second door to the left, down that corridor. (PHILLIPSON departs.) Good evening to you, Mr.—ah—Mr.—?

UNDERSHELL - (coming forward). Mr. Undershell. Lady Culverin expects me, I believe.

TREDWELL - Quite correct, Mr. Undershell, sir. She do. Leastwise, I shouldn't say myself she'd require to see you—well, not before to-morrow morning—but you won't mind that, I dare say.

UNDERSHELL - (choking). Not mind that! Take me to her at once!

TREDWELL - Couldn't take it on myself, sir, really. There's no particular 'urry. I'll let her ladyship know you're 'ere; and if she wants you, she'll send for you; but, with a party staying in the 'ouse, and others dining with us to-night, it ain't likely as she'll have time for you till to-morrow.

UNDERSHELL - Oh, then whenever her ladyship should find leisure to recollect my existence, will you have the goodness to inform her that I have taken the liberty of returning to town by the next train?

TREDWELL - Lor! Mr. Undershell, you aren't so pressed as all that, are you? I know my lady wouldn't like you to go without seeing you personally; no more wouldn't Sir Rupert Culverin. And I understood you was coming down for the Sunday!

UNDERSHELL - (furious). So did I—but not to be treated like this!

TREDWELL - (soothingly). Why, you know what ladies are. And you couldn't see Deerfoot—not properly, to-night, either.

UNDERSHELL - I have seen enough of this place already. I intend to go back by the next train, I tell you.

TREDWELL - But there ain't any next train up to-night—being a loop line—not to mention that I've sent the fly away, and they can't spare no one at the stables to drive you in. Come, sir, make the best of it. I've had my horders to see that you're made comfortable, and Mrs. Pomfret and me will expect the pleasure of your company at supper in the 'ousekeeper's room, 9.30 sharp. I'll send the steward's room boy to show you to your room.

[He goes, leaving UNDERSHELL speechless.

UNDERSHELL - (almost foaming). The insolence of these cursed aristocrats! Lady Culverin will see me when she has time, forsooth! I am to be entertained in the servants' hall! This is how our upper classes honour Poetry! I won't stay a single hour under their infernal roof. I'll walk. But where to? And how about my luggage?

[PHILLIPSON returns.

PHILLIPSON - Mr. Tredwell says you want to go already! It can't be true! Without even waiting for supper?

UNDERSHELL - (gloomily). Why should I wait for supper in this house?

PHILLIPSON - Well, I shall be there; I don't know if that's any inducement.

[She looks down.

UNDERSHELL - (to himself). She is a singularly bewitching creature; and I'm starving. Why shouldn't I stay—if only to shame these Culverins? It will be an experience—a study in life. I can always go afterwards. I will stay. (Aloud.) You little know the sacrifice you ask of me, but enough; I give way. We shall meet—(with a gulp)—in the housekeeper's room!

PHILLIPSON - (highly amused). You are a comical little man. You'll be the death of me if you go on like that!

[She flits away.

UNDERSHELL - (alone). I feel disposed to be the death of somebody! Oh, Lady Maisie Mull, to what a bathos have you lured your poet by your artless flattery—a banquet presided over by your aunt's butler!

## PART VII

The Amber Boudoir at Wyvern immediately after LADY CANTIRE and her daughter have entered.

LADY CANTIRE - (in reply to LADY CULVERIN). Tea? oh yes, my dear; anything warm! I'm positively perished—that tedious cold journey and the long drive afterwards! I always tell Rupert he would see me far oftener at Wyvern if he would only get the company to bring the line round close to the park gates, but it has no effect upon him! (As TREDWELL announces SPURRELL, who enters in trepidation.) Mr. James Spurrell! Who's Mr.—? Oh, to be sure; that's the name of my interesting young poet— Andromeda, you know, my dear! Go and be pleasant to him, Albinia, he wants reassuring.

LADY CULERIN - (a trifle nervous). How do you do, Mr.—ah—Spurrell? (To herself.) I said he ended in "ell"! (Aloud.) So pleased to see you! We think so much of your Andromeda here, you know. Quite delightful of you to find time to run down!

SPURRELL - (to himself). Why, she's chummy, too! Old Drummy pulls me through everything! (Aloud.) Don't name it, my la—hum—Lady Culverin - No trouble at all; only too proud to get your summons!

LADY CULERIN - (to herself). He doesn't seem very revolutionary! (Aloud.) That's so sweet of you; when so many must be absolutely fighting to get you!

SPURRELL - Oh, as for that, there is rather a run on me just now, but I put everything else aside for you, of course!

LADY CULERIN - (to herself). He's soon reassured. (Aloud, with a touch of frost.) I am sure we must consider ourselves most fortunate. (Turning to the COUNTESS.) You did say cream, Rohesia? Sugar, Maisie dearest?

SPURRELL - (to himself). I'm all right up to now! I suppose I'd better say nothing about the horse till they do. I feel rather out of it among these nobs, though. I'll try and chum on to little Lady Maisie again; she may have got over her temper by this time, and she's the only one I know. (He approaches her.) Well, Lady Maisie, here I am, you see. I'd really no idea your aunt would be so friendly! I say, you know, you don't mind speaking to a fellow, do you? I've no one else I can go to—and—and it's a bit strange at first, you know!

LADY MAISIE - (colouring with mingled apprehension, vexation, and pity). If I can be of any help to you, Mr. Spurrell—!

SPURRELL - Well, if you'd only tell me what I ought to do!

LADY MAISIE - Surely that's very simple; do nothing; just take everything quietly as it comes, and you can't make any mistakes.

SPURRELL - (anxiously). And you don't think anybody'll see anything out of the way in my being here like this?

LADY MAISIE - (to herself). I'm only too afraid they will! (Aloud.) You really must have a little self-confidence. Just remember that no one here could produce anything a millionth part as splendid as your Andromeda! It's too distressing to see you so appallingly humble! (To herself.) There's Captain Thicknesse over there—he might come and rescue me; but he doesn't seem to care to!

SPURRELL - Well, you do put some heart into me, Lady Maisie. I feel equal to the lot of 'em now!

PILLINER - (to MISS SPELWANE) Is that the poet? Why, but I say—he's a fraud! Where's his matted head? He's not a bit ragged, or rusty either. And why don't he dabble? Don't seem to know what to do with his hands quite, though, does he?

MISS SPELWANE - (coldly). He knows how to do some very exquisite poetry with one of them, at all events. I've been reading it, and I think it perfectly marvellous!

PILLINER - I see what it is, you're preparing to turn his matted head for him? I warn you you'll only waste your sweetness. That pretty little Lady Maisie's annexed him. Can't you content yourself with one victim at a time?

MISS SPELWANE - Don't be so utterly idiotic! (To herself.) If Maisie imagines she's to be allowed to monopolise the only man in the room worth talking to!—

CAPTAIN THICKNESSE - (to himself, as he watches Lady MAISIE). She is lookin' prettier than ever! Forgotten me. Used to be friendly enough once, though, till her mother warned me off. Seems to have a good deal to say to that poet fellow; saw her colour up from here the moment he came near; he's begun Petrarchin', hang him! I'd cross over and speak to her if I could catch her eye. Don't know, though; what's the use? She wouldn't thank me for interruptin'. She likes these clever chaps; don't signify to her if they are bounders, I suppose. I'm not intellectual. Gad, I wish I'd gone back to Aldershot!

LADY CANTIRE - (by the tea-table). Why don't you make that woman of yours send you up decent cakes, my dear? These are cinders. I'm afraid you let her have too much of her own way. Now, tell me—who are your party? Vivien Spelwane! Never have that girl to meet me again, I can't endure her; and that affected little ape of a Mr. Pilliner—h'm! Do I see Captain Thicknesse? Now, I don't object to him. Maisie and he used to be great friends.... Ah, how do you do, Captain Thicknesse? Quite pleasant finding you here; such ages since we saw anything of you! Why haven't you been near us all this time?... Oh, I may have been out once or twice when you called; but you might have tried again, mightn't you? There, I forgive you; you had better go and see if you can make your peace with Maisie!

CAPTAIN THICKNESSE - (to himself, as he obeys). Doosid odd, Lady Cantire comin' round like this. Wish she'd thought of it before.

LADY CANTIRE - (in a whisper). He's always been such a favourite of mine. They tell me his uncle, poor dear Lord Dunderhead, is so ill—felt the loss of his only son so terribly. Of course it will make a great difference—in many ways.

CAPTAIN THICKNESSE - (constrainedly to LADY MAISIE). How do you do? Afraid you've forgotten me.

LADY MAISIE - Oh no, indeed! (Hurriedly.) You—you don't know Mr. Spurrell, I think? (Introducing them.) Captain Thicknesse.

CAPTAIN THICKNESSE - How are you? Been hearin' a lot about you lately. Andromeda, don't you know; and that kind of thing.

SPURRELL - It's wonderful what a hit she seems to have made—not that I'm surprised at it, either; I always knew—

LADY MAISIE - (hastily) Oh, Mr. Spurrell, you haven't had any tea! Do go and get some before it's taken away.

[SPURRELL goes.

CAPTAIN THICKNESSE - Been tryin' to get you to notice me ever since you came; but you were so awfully absorbed, you know!

LADY MAISIE - Was I? So absorbed as all that! What with?

CAPTAIN THICKNESSE - Well, it looked like it—with talkin' to your poetical friend.

LADY MAISIE - (flushing). He is not my friend in particular; I—I admire his poetry, of course.

CAPTAIN THICKNESSE - (to himself). Can't even speak of him without a change of colour. Bad sign that! (Aloud.) You always were keen about poetry and literature and that in the old days, weren't you? Used to rag me for not readin' enough. But I do now. I was readin' a book only last week. I'll tell you the name if you give me a minute to think—book everybody's readin' just now—no end of a clever book.

[Miss SPELWANE rushes across to Lady MAISIE.

MISS SPELWANE - Maisie, dear, how are you? You look so tired! That's the journey, I suppose. (Whispering.) Do tell me—is that really the author of Andromeda drinking tea close by? You're a great friend of his, I know. Do be a dear, and introduce him to me! I declare the dogs have made friends with him already. Poets have such a wonderful attraction for animals, haven't they?

[LADY MAISIE has to bring SPURRELL up and introduce him; CAPTAIN THICKNESSE chooses to consider himself dismissed.

MISS SPELWANE - (with shy adoration). Oh, Mr. Spurrell, I feel as if I must talk to you about Andromeda. I did so admire it!

SPURRELL - (to himself). Another of 'em! They seem uncommonly sweet on "bulls" in this house! (Aloud.) Very glad to hear you say so, I'm sure. But I'm bound to say she's about as near perfection as anything I ever—I dare say you went over her points—

MISS SPELWANE - Indeed, I believe none of them were lost upon me; but my poor little praise must seem so worthless and ignorant!

SPURRELL - (indulgently). Oh, I wouldn't say that. I find some ladies very knowing about these things. I'm having a picture done of her.

MISS SPELWANE - Are you really? How delightful! As a frontispiece?

SPURRELL - Eh? Oh no—full length, and sideways—so as to show her legs, you know.

MISS SPELWANE - Her legs? Oh, of course—with "her roseal toes cramped." I thought that such a wonderful touch!

SPURRELL - They're not more cramped than they ought to be; she never turned them in, you know!

MISS SPELWANE - (mystified). I didn't suppose she did. And now tell me—if it's not an indiscreet question—when do you expect there'll be another edition?

SPURRELL – (to himself). Another addition! She's cadging for a pup now! (Aloud.) Oh—er—really—couldn't say.

MISS SPELWANE - I'm sure the first must be disposed of by this time. I shall look out for the next so eagerly!

SPURRELL - (to himself). Time I "off"ed it. (Aloud.) Afraid I can't say anything definite—and, excuse me leaving you, but I think Lady Culverin is looking my way.

MISS SPELWANE - Oh, by all means? (To herself.) I might as well praise a pillar-post! And after spending quite half an hour reading him up, too! I wonder if Bertie Pilliner was right; but I shall have him all to myself at dinner.

LADY CANTIRE - And where is Rupert? too busy of course to come and say a word! Well, some day he may understand what a sister is—when it's too late. Ah, here's our nice unassuming young poet coming up to talk to you. Don't repel him, my dear!

SPURRELL - (to himself). Better give her the chance of telling me what's wrong with the horse, I suppose. (Aloud.) Er—nice old-fashioned sort of house this, Lady Culverin (To himself.) I'll work round to the stabling by degrees.

LADY CULERIN - (coldly). I believe it dates from the Tudors—if that is what you mean.

LADY CANTIRE - My dear Albinia, I quite understand him; "old-fashioned" is exactly the epithet. And I was born and brought up here, so perhaps I should know.

[A FOOTMAN enters, and comes up to SPURRELL mysteriously.

FOOTMAN - Will you let me have your keys, if you please, sir?

SPURRELL - (in some alarm). My keys! (Suspiciously.) Why, what do you want them for?

LADY CANTIRE - (in a whisper). Isn't he deliciously unsophisticated? Quite a child of nature! (Aloud.) My dear Mr. Spurrell, he wants your keys to unlock your portmanteau and put out your things; you'll be able to dress for dinner all the quicker.

SPURRELL - Do you mean—am I to have the honour of sitting down to table with all of you?

LADY CULERIN - (to herself). Oh, my goodness, what will Rupert say? (Aloud.) Why, of course, Mr. Spurrell; how can you ask?

SPURRELL - (feebly). I—I didn't know, that was all. (To FOOTMAN.) Here you are, then. (To himself.) Put out my things?—he'll find nothing to put out except a nightgown, sponge bag, and a couple of brushes! If I'd only known I should be let in for this, I'd have brought dress-clothes. But how could I? I—I wonder if it would be any good telling 'em quietly how it is. I shouldn't like 'em to think I hadn't got any. (He looks at Lady Cantire and her sister-in-law, who are talking in an undertone.) No, perhaps I'd better let it alone. I—I can allude to it in a joky sort of way when I come down!

PART VIII

SURPRISES—AGREEABLE AND OTHERWISE

In the Amber Boudoir. SIR RUPERT has just entered.

SIR RUPERT CULVERIN - Ha, Maisie, my dear, glad to see you! Well, Rohesia, how are you, eh? You're looking uncommonly well! No idea you were here!

SPURRELL - (to himself). Sir Rupert! He'll hoof me out of this pretty soon, I expect!

LADY CANTIRE - (aggrieved). We have been in the house for the best part of an hour, Rupert—as you might have discovered by inquiring—but no doubt you preferred your comfort to welcoming so unimportant a guest as your sister!

SIR RUPERT CULVERIN - (to himself). Beginning already! (Aloud.) Very sorry—got rather wet riding—had to change everything. And I knew Albinia was here.

LADY CANTIRE - (magnanimously). Well, we won't begin to quarrel the moment we meet; and you are forgetting your other guest. (In an undertone.) Mr. Spurrell—the poet—wrote Andromeda. (Aloud.) Mr. Spurrell, come and let me present you to my brother.

SIR RUPERT CULVERIN - Ah, how d'ye do? (To himself, as he shakes hands.) What the deuce am I to say to this fellow? (Aloud.) Glad to see you here, Mr. Spurrell—heard all about you—Andromeda, eh? Hope you'll manage to amuse yourself while you're with us; afraid there's not much you can do now though.

SPURRELL - (to himself). Horse in a bad way; time they let me see it. (Aloud.) Well, we must see, sir; I'll do all I can.

SIR RUPERT CULVERIN - You see, the shooting's done now.

SPURRELL - (to himself, professionally piqued). They might have waited till I'd seen the horse before they shot him! After calling me in like this! (Aloud.) Oh, I'm sorry to hear that, Sir. I wish I could have got here earlier, I'm sure.

SIR RUPERT CULVERIN - Wish we'd asked you a month ago, if you're fond of shooting. Thought you might look down on sport, perhaps.

SPURRELL - (to himself). Sport? Why, he's talking of birds—not the horse! (Aloud.) Me, Sir Rupert? Not much! I'm as keen on a day's gunning as any man, though I don't often get the chance now.

SIR RUPERT CULVERIN - (to himself, pleased). Come, he don't seem strong against the Game Laws! (Aloud.) Thought you didn't look as if you sat over your desk all day! There's hunting still, of course. Don't know whether you ride?

SPURRELL - Rather so, sir! Why, I was born and bred in a sporting county, and as long as my old uncle was alive, I could go down to his farm and get a run with the hounds now and again.

SIR RUPERT CULVERIN - (delighted). Capital! Well, our next meet is on Tuesday—best part of the country; nearly all grass, and nice clean post and rails. You must stay over for it. Got a mare that will carry your weight perfectly, and I think I can promise you a run—eh, what do you say?

SPURRELL - (to himself, in surprise). He is a chummy old cock! I'll wire old Spavin that I'm detained on biz; and I'll tell 'em to send my riding-breeches and dress-clothes down! (Aloud.) It's uncommonly kind of you, sir, and I think I can manage to stop on a bit.

LADY CULERIN - (to herself). Rupert must be out of his senses! It's bad enough to have him here till Monday! (Aloud.) We mustn't forget, Rupert, how valuable Mr. Spurrell's time is; it would be too selfish of us to detain him here a day longer than—

LADY CANTIRE - My dear, Mr. Spurrell has already said he can manage it; so we may all enjoy his society with a clear conscience. (LADY CULVERIN conceals her sentiments with difficulty.) And now, Albinia, if you'll excuse me, I think I'll go to my room and rest a little, as I'm rather overdone, and you have all these tiresome people coming to dinner to-night.

[She rises and leaves the room; the other ladies follow her example.

LADY CULVERIN - Rupert, I'm going up now with Rohesia. You know where we've put Mr. Spurrell, don't you? The Verney Chamber.

[She goes out.

SIR RUPERT CULVERIN - Take you up now, if you like, Mr. Spurrell—it's only just seven, though. Suppose you don't take an hour to dress, eh?

SPURRELL - Oh dear no, sir, nothing like it! (To himself.) Won't take me two minutes as I am now! I'd better tell him—I can say my bag hasn't come. I don't believe it has, and, anyway, it's a good excuse. (Aloud.) The—the fact is, Sir Rupert, I'm afraid that my luggage has been unfortunately left behind.

SIR RUPERT CULVERIN - No luggage, eh? Well, well, it's of no consequence. But I'll ask about it—I dare say it's all right.

[He goes out.

CAPTAIN THICKNESSE - (to SPURRELL). Sure to have turned up, you know—man will have seen that. Shouldn't altogether object to a glass of sherry and bitters before dinner. Don't know how you feel—suppose you've a soul above sherry and bitters, though?

SPURRELL - Not at this moment. But I'd soon put my soul above a sherry and bitters if I got a chance!

CAPTAIN THICKNESSE - (after reflection). I say, you know, that's rather smart, eh? (To himself.) Aw'fly clever sort of chap, this, but not stuck up—not half a bad sort, if he is a bit of a bounder. (Aloud.) Anythin' in the evenin' paper? Don't get 'em down here.

SPURRELL - Nothing much. I see there's an objection to Monkey-tricks.

CAPTAIN THICKNESSE - (startled). No, by Jove! Hope they'll overrule it—make a lot of difference to me if they don't.

SPURRELL - Don't fancy there's much in it. Your money's safe enough, I expect. Have you any particular fancy for the Grand National? I know something that's safe to win, bar accidents—a dead cert, sir! Got the tip straight from the stable. You just take my advice, and pile all you can on Jumping Joan.

CAPTAIN THICKNESSE - (later, to himself, after a long and highly interesting conversation). Thunderin' clever chap—never knew poets were such clever chaps. Might be a "bookie," by Gad! No wonder Maisie thinks such a lot of him!

[He sighs.

SIR RUPERT CULVERIN - (returning). Now, Mr. Spurrell, if you'll come upstairs with me, I'll show you your quarters. By the way, I've made inquiries about your luggage, and I think you'll find it's all right. (As he leads the way up the staircase.) Rather awkward for you if you'd had to come down to dinner just as you are, eh?

SPURRELL - (to himself). Oh, lor, my beastly bag has come after all! Now they'll know I didn't bring a dress suit. What an owl I was to tell him! (Aloud, feebly.) Oh—er—very awkward indeed, Sir Rupert!

SIR RUPERT CULVERIN - (stopping at a bedroom door). Verney Chamber—here you are. Ah, my wife forgot to have your name put on the door—better do it now, eh? (He writes it on the card in the door-plate.) There—well, hope you'll find it all comfortable—we dine at eight, you know. You've plenty of time for all you've got to do!

SPURRELL - (to himself). If I only knew what to do! I shall never have the cheek to come down as I am!

[He enters the Verney Chamber dejectedly.

In an Upper Corridor in the East Wing.

STEWARD'S ROOM BOY - (to UNDERSHELL). This is your room, sir—you'll find a fire lit and all.

UNDERSHELL - (scathingly). A fire? For me! I scarcely expected such an indulgence. You are sure there's no mistake?

STEWARD'S ROOM BOY - This is the room I was told, sir. You'll find candles on the mantelpiece, and matches.

UNDERSHELL - Every luxury indeed! I am pampered—pampered!

STEWARD'S ROOM BOY - Yes, sir. And I was to say as supper's at ar-past nine, but Mrs. Pomfret would be 'appy to see you in the Pugs' Parlour whenever you pleased to come down and set there.

UNDERSHELL - The Pugs' Parlour?

STEWARD'S ROOM BOY - What we call the 'ousekeeper's room, among ourselves, sir.

UNDERSHELL - Mrs. Pomfret does me too much honour. And shall I have the satisfaction of seeing your intelligent countenance at the festive board, my lad?

STEWARD'S ROOM BOY - (giggling). On'y to wait, sir. I don't set down to meals along with the upper servants, sir!

UNDERSHELL - And I—a mere man of genius—do! These distinctions must strike you as most arbitrary; but restrain any natural envy, my young friend. I assure you I am not puffed up by this promotion!

STEWARD'S ROOM BOY - No, sir. (To himself, as he goes out.) I believe he's a bit dotty, I do. I don't understand a word he's been a-talking of!

UNDERSHELL - (alone, surveying the surroundings). A cockloft, with a painted iron bedstead, a smoky chimney, no bell, and a text over the mantelpiece! Thank Heaven, that fellow Drysdale can't see me here! But I will not sleep in this place, my pride will only just bear the strain of staying to supper—no more. And I'm hanged if I go down to the housekeeper's room till hunger drives me. It's not eight yet—how shall I pass the time? Ha, I see they've favoured me with pen and ink. I will invoke the Muse. Indignation should make verses, as it did for Juvenal; and he was never set down to sup with slaves!

[He writes.

In the Verney Chamber.

SPURRELL - (to himself). My word, what a room! Carpet hung all over the walls, big fourposter, carved ceiling, great fireplace with blazing logs,—if this is how they do a vet here, what price the other fellows' rooms? And to think I shall have to do without dinner, just when I was getting on with 'em all so swimmingly! I must. I can't, for the credit of the profession—to say nothing of the firm—turn up in a monkey jacket and tweed bags, and that's all I've got except a nightgown!... It's all very well for Lady Maisie to say, "Take everything as it comes," but if she was in my fix!... And it isn't as if I hadn't got dress things either. If only I'd brought 'em down, I'd have marched in to dinner as cool as a— (he lights a pair of candles.) Hullo! What's that on the bed? (He approaches it.) Shirt! white tie! socks! coat, waistcoat, trousers—they are dress clothes!... And here's a pair of brushes on the table! I'll swear they're not mine—there's a monogram on them—"U.G." What does it all mean? Why, of course! regular old trump, Sir Rupert, and naturally he wants me to do him credit. He saw how it was, and he's gone and rigged me out! In a house like this, they're ready for emergencies—keep all sizes in stock, I dare say.... It isn't "U.G." on the brushes—it's "G.U."—"Guest's Use." Well, this is what I call doing the thing in style! Cinderella's nothing to it! Only hope they're a decent fit. (Later, as he dresses.) Come, the shirt's all right; trousers a trifle short—but they'll let down; waistcoat—whew, must undo the buckle—hang it, it is undone! I feel like a hooped barrel in it! Now the coat—easy does it. Well, it's on; but I shall have to be peeled like a walnut to get it off again.... Shoes? ah, here they are—pair of pumps. Phew—must have come from the Torture Exhibition in Leicester Square; glass slippers nothing to 'em! But they'll have to do at a pinch; and they do pinch like blazes! Ha, ha, that's good! I must tell that to the Captain. (He looks at himself in a mirror.) Well, I can't say they're up to mine for cut and general style; but they're passable. And now I'll go down to the drawing-room and get on terms with all the smarties!

[He saunters out with restored complacency.

PART IX

THE MAUVAIS QUART D'HEURE

In the Chinese Drawing-room at Wyvern.

TIME—7.50. LADY CULVERIN is alone, glancing over a written list.

LADY CANTIRE - (entering). Down already, Albinia? I thought if I made haste I should get a quiet chat with you before anybody else came in. What is that paper? Oh, the list of couples for Rupert. May I see? (As LADY CULVERIN surrenders it.) My dear, you're not going to inflict that mincing little Pilliner boy on poor Maisie! That really won't do. At least let her have somebody she used to. Why not Captain Thicknesse? He's an old friend, and she's not seen him for months. I must alter that, if you've no objection. (She does.) And then you've given my poor poet to that Spelwane girl! Now, why?

LADY CULVERIN - I thought she wouldn't mind putting up with him just for one evening.

LADY CANTIRE - Wouldn't mind! Putting up with him! And is that how you speak of a celebrity when you are so fortunate as to have one to entertain? Really, Albinia!

LADY CULVERIN - But, my dear Rohesia, you must allow that, whatever his talents may be, he is not—well, not quite one of Us. Now, is he?

LADY CANTIRE - (blandly) My dear, I never heard he had any connection with the manufacture of chemical manures, in which your worthy papa so greatly distinguished himself—if that is what you mean.

LADY CULERIN - (with some increase of colour). That is not what I meant, Rohesia—as you know perfectly well. And I do say that this Mr. Spurrell's manner is most objectionable; when he's not obsequious, he's horribly familiar!

LADY CANTIRE - (sharply). I have not observed it. He strikes me as well enough—for that class of person. And it is intellect, soul, all that kind of thing that I value. I look below the surface, and I find a great deal that is very original and charming in this young man. And surely, my dear, if I find myself able to associate with him, you need not be so fastidious! I consider him my protégé, and I won't have him slighted. He is far too good for Vivien Spelwane!

LADY CULERIN - (with just a suspicion of malice). Perhaps, Rohesia, you would like him to take you in?

LADY CANTIRE - That, of course, is quite out of the question. I see you have given me the Bishop—he's a poor, dry stick of a man—never forgets he was the Headmaster of Swisham—but he's always glad to meet me. I freshen him up so.

LADY CULVERIN - I really don't know whom I can give Mr. Spurrell. There's Rhoda Cokayne, but she's not poetical, and she'll get on much better with Archie Bearpark. Oh, I forgot Mrs. Brooke-Chatteris—she's sure to talk, at all events.

LADY CANTIRE - (as she corrects the list). A lively, agreeable woman—she'll amuse him. Now you can give Rupert the list.

[SIR RUPERT and various members of the house-party appear one by one; LORD and LADY LULLINGTON, the BISHOP of BIRCHESTER and MRS RODNEY, MR and MRS EARWAKER, and MR SHORTHORN are announced at intervals; salutations, recognitions, and commonplaces are exchanged.

LADY CANTIRE - (later—to the Bishop, genially). Ah, my dear Bishop, you and I haven't met since we had our great battle about—now, was it the necessity of throwing open the Public Schools to the lower classes—for whom of course they were originally intended—or was it the failure of the Church to reach the working man? I really forget.

The Bishop (who has a holy horror of the Countess). I—ah—fear I cannot charge my memory so precisely, my dear Lady Cantire. We—ah—differ unfortunately on so many subjects. I trust, however, we may—ah—agree to suspend hostilities on this occasion?

LADY CANTIRE - (with even more bonhomie). Don't be too sure of that, Bishop. I've several crows to pluck with you, and we are to go in to dinner together, you know!

THE BISHOP - Indeed? I had no conception that such a pleasure was in store for me! (To himself.) This must be the penance for breaking my rule of never dining out on Saturday! Severe—but not unmerited!

LADY CANTIRE - I wonder, Bishop, if you have seen this wonderful volume of poetry that every one is talking about—Andromeda?

THE BISHOP - (conscientiously). I chanced only this morning, by way of momentary relaxation, to take up a journal containing a notice of that work, with copious extracts. The impression left on my mind was—ah—unfavourable; a certain talent, no doubt, some felicity of expression, but a noticeable lack of the—ah—reticence, the discipline, the—the scholarly touch which a training at one of our great Public Schools (I forbear to particularise), and at a University, can alone impart. I was also pained to observe a crude discontent with the existing Social System—a system which, if not absolutely perfect, cannot be upset or even modified without the gravest danger. But I was still more distressed to note in several passages a decided taint of the morbid sensuousness which renders so much of our modern literature sickly and unwholesome.

LADY CANTIRE - All prejudice, my dear Bishop; why, you haven't even read the book! However, the author is staying here now, and I feel convinced that if you only knew him, you'd alter your opinion. Such an unassuming, inoffensive creature! There, he's just come in. I'll call him over here.... Goodness, why does he shuffle along in that way!

SPURRELL - (meeting SIR RUPERT). Hope I've kept nobody waiting for me, Sir Rupert Culverin. (Confidentially.) I'd rather a job to get these things on; but they're really a wonderful fit, considering!

[He passes on, leaving his host speechless.

LADY CANTIRE - That's right, Mr. Spurell. Come here, and let me present you to the Bishop of Birchester. The Bishop has just been telling me he considers your Andromeda sickly, or unhealthy, or something. I'm sure you'll be able to convince him it's nothing of the sort.

[She leaves him with THE BISHOP, who is visibly annoyed.

SPURRELL - (to himself, overawed). Oh, Lor! Wish I knew the right way to talk to a Bishop. Can't call him nothing—so doosid familiar. (Aloud.) Andromeda sickly, your—(tentatively)—your Right Reverence? Not a bit of it—sound as a roach!

THE BISHOP - If I had thought my—ah—criticisms were to be repeated—I might say misrepresented, as the Countess has thought proper to do, Mr. Spurrell, I should not have ventured to make them. At the same time, you must be conscious yourself, I think, of certain blemishes which would justify the terms I employed.

SPURRELL - I never saw any in Andromeda myself, your—your Holiness. You're the first to find a fault in her. I don't say there mayn't be something dicky about the setting and the turn of the tail, but that's a trifle.

THE BISHOP - I did not refer to the setting of the tale, and the portions I object to are scarcely trifles. But pardon me if I prefer to end a discussion that can hardly be other than unprofitable. (To himself, as he turns on his heel.) A most arrogant, self-satisfied, and conceited young man—a truly lamentable product of this half-educated age!

SPURRELL - (to himself). Well, he may be a dab at dogmas—he don't know much about dogs. Drummy's got a constitution worth a dozen of his!

LADY CULERIN - (approaching him). Oh, Mr. Spurrell, Lord Lullington is most anxious to know you. If you will come with me. (To herself, as she leads him up to LORD LULLINGTON.) I do wish Rohesia wouldn't force me to do this sort of thing!

[She presents him.

LORD LULLINGTON - (to himself). I suppose I ought to know all about his novel, or whatever it is he's done. (Aloud, with courtliness.) Very pleased to make your acquaintance, Mr. Spurrell; you've—ah—delighted the world by your Andromeda. When are we to look for your next production? Soon, I hope.

SPURRELL - (to himself). He's after a pup now! Never met such a doggy lot in my life! (Aloud.) Er—well, my lord, I've promised so many as it is, that I hardly see my way to—

LORD LULLINGTON - (paternally) Take my advice, my dear young man, leave yourself as free as possible. Expect you to give us your best, you know.

[He turns to continue a conversation.

SPURRELL - (to himself). Give it! He won't get it under a five-pound note, I can tell him. (He makes his way to Miss SPELWANE.) I say, what do you think the old Bishop's been up to? Pitching into Andromeda like the very dooce—says she's sickly!

MISS SPELWANE - (to herself). He brings his literary disappointments to me, not Maisie! (Aloud, with the sweetest sympathy.) How dreadfully unjust! Oh, I've dropped my fan—no, pray don't trouble; I can pick it up. My arms are so long, you know—like a kangaroo's—no, what is that animal which has such long arms? You're so clever, you ought to know!

SPURRELL - I suppose you mean a gorilla?

MISS SPELWANE - How crushing of you! But you must go away now, or else you'll find nothing to say to me at dinner—you take me in, you know. I hope you feel privileged. I feel— But if I told you, I might make you too conceited!

SPURRELL - (gracefully). Oh, it's not so easily done as all that!

[Sir RUPERT approaches with MR SHORTHORN.

SIR RUPERT CULVERIN - Vivien, my dear, let me introduce Mr. Shorthorn—Miss Spelwane. (To SPURRELL.) Let me see—ha—yes, you take in Mrs. Chatteris. Don't know her? Come this way, and I'll find her for you.

[He marches SPURRELL off.

MR SHORTHORN - (to MISS SPELWANE). Good thing getting this rain at last; a little more of this dry weather and we should have had no grass to speak of!

MISS SPELWANE - (who has not quite recovered from her disappointment). And now you will have some grass to speak of? How fortunate!

SPURRELL - (as dinner is announced, to Lady MAISIE). I say, Lady Maisie, I've just been told I've got to take in a married lady. I don't know what to talk to her about. I should feel a lot more at home with you. Couldn't we work it somehow?

LADY MAISIE - (to herself). What a fearful suggestion—but I simply daren't snub him! (Aloud.) I'm afraid, Mr. Spurrell, we must both put up with the partners we have; most distressing, isn't it—but!

[She gives a little shrug.

CAPTAIN THICKNESSE - (immediately behind her, to himself). Gad, that's pleasant! I knew I'd better have gone to Aldershot! (Aloud.) I've been told off to take you in, Lady Maisie—not my fault, don't you know.

LADY MAISIE - There's no need to be so apologetic about it. (To herself.) Oh, I hope he didn't hear what I said to that wretch!

CAPTAIN THICKNESSE - Well, I rather thought there might be, perhaps.

LADY MAISIE - (to herself). He did hear it. If he's going to be so stupid as to misunderstand, I'm sure I shan't explain.

[They take their place in the procession to the dining-hall.


PART X

BORROWED PLUMES

In UNDERSHELL'S Bedroom in the East Wing at Wyvern.

TIME—About 9 P.M.

THE STEWARD'S ROOM BOY - (knocking and entering). Brought you up some 'ot water, sir, case you'd like to clean up afore supper.

UNDERSHELL - I presume evening dress is not indispensable in the housekeeper's room; but I can hardly make even the simplest toilet until you are good enough to bring up my portmanteau. Where is it?

THE STEWARD'S ROOM BOY - I never 'eard nothink of no porkmanteau, sir!

UNDERSHELL - You will hear a good deal about it, unless it is forthcoming at once. Just find out what's become of it—a new portmanteau, with a white star painted on it.

[THE STEWARD'S ROOM BOY retires, impressed. An interval.

THE STEWARD'S ROOM BOY - (reappearing). I managed to get a few words with Thomas, our second footman, just as he was coming out o' the 'all, and he sez the only porkmanteau with a white star was took up to the Verney Chamber, which Thomas unpacked it hisself.

UNDERSHELL - Then tell Thomas, with my compliments, that he will trouble himself to pack it again immediately.

THE STEWARD'S ROOM BOY - But Thomas has to wait at table, and besides, he says as he laid out the dress things, and the gen'lman as is in the Verney Chamber is a wearin' of 'em now, sir.

UNDERSHELL - (indignant). But they're mine! Confound his impudence! Here, I'll write him a line at once. (He scribbles a note.) There, see that the gentleman of the Verney Chamber gets this at once, and bring me his answer.

THE STEWARD'S ROOM BOY - What! me go into the dinin'-'all, with all the swells at table? I dursn't. I should get the sack from old Treddy.

UNDERSHELL - I don't care who takes it so long as it is taken. Tell Thomas it's his mistake, and he must do what he can to put it right. Say I shall certainly complain if I don't get back my clothes and portmanteau. Get that note delivered somehow, and I'll give you half-a-crown. (To himself, as the Boy departs, much against his will.) If Lady Culverin doesn't consider me fit to appear at her dinner-table, I don't see why my evening clothes should be more privileged!

In the Dining-hall. The table is oval; SPURRELL is placed between LADY RHONDA COKAYNE and MRS BROOKE-CHATTERIS.

MRS CHATTERIS - (encouragingly, after they are seated). Now, I shall expect you to be very brilliant and entertaining. I'll do all the listening for once in a way—though, generally, I can talk about all manner of silly things with anybody!

SPURRELL - (extremely ill at ease). Oh—er—I should say you were quite equal to that. But I really can't think of anything to talk about.

MRS CHATTERIS - That's a bad beginning. I always find the menu cards such a good subject, when there's anything at all out of the common about them. If they're ornamented, you can talk about them—though not for very long at a time, don't you think?

SPURRELL - (miserably). I can't say how long I could go on about ornamented ones—but these are plain. (To himself.) I can hear this waistcoat going already—and we're only at the soup!

MRS CHATTERIS - It is a pity. Never mind; tell me about literary and artistic people. Do you know, I'm rather glad I'm not literary or artistic myself; it seems to make people so queer-looking, somehow. Oh, of course I didn't mean you looked queer—but generally, you know. You've made quite a success with your Andromeda, haven't you? I only go by what I'm told—I don't read much myself. We women have so many really serious matters to attend to—arranging about dinners, and visits, and trying on frocks, and then rushing about from party to party. I so seldom get a quiet moment. Ah, I knew I wanted to ask you something. Did you ever know any one called Lady Grisoline?

SPURRELL - Lady—er—Grisoline? No; can't say I do. I know Lady Maisie, that's all.

MRS CHATTERIS - Oh, and she was the original? Now, that is exciting! But I should hardly have recognised her—"lanky," you know, and "slanting green eyes." But I suppose you see everybody differently from other people? It's having so much imagination. I dare say I look green or something to you now—though really I'm not.

SPURRELL - (to himself). I don't understand more than about half she's saying. (Aloud.) Oh, I don't see anything particularly green about you.

MRS CHATTERIS - (only partially pleased). I wonder if you meant that to be complimentary—no, you needn't explain. Now, tell me, is there any news about the Laureateship? Who's going to get it? Will it be Swinburne or Lewis Morris?

SPURRELL - (to himself). Never heard of the stakes or the horses either. (Aloud.) Well, to tell you the truth, I haven't been following their form—too many of these small events nowadays.

MRS CHATTERIS - (to herself). It's quite amusing how jealous these poets are of one another! (Aloud.) Is it true they get a butt of sherry given them for it?

SPURRELL - I've heard of winners getting a bottle or two of champagne in a bucket—not sherry. But a little stimulant won't hurt a crack when he comes in, provided it's not given him too soon; wait till he's got his wind and done blowing, you know.

MRS CHATTERIS - I'm taking that in. I know it's very witty and satirical, and I dare say I shall understand it in time.

SPURRELL - Oh, it doesn't matter much if you don't. (To himself.) Pleasant kind of woman—but a perfect fool to talk to!

MRS CHATTERIS - (to herself). I've always heard that clever writers are rather stupid when you meet them—it's quite true.

CAPTAIN THICKNESSE - (to himself). I should like her to see that I've got some imagination in me, though she does think me such an ass. (Aloud, to Lady MAISIE.) Jolly old hall this is, with the banners, and the gallery, and that—makes you fancy some of those old mediæval Johnnies in armour—knights, you know—comin' clankin' in and turnin' us all out.

LADY MAISIE - (to herself). I do trust Mr. Spurrell isn't saying something too dreadful. I'm sure I heard my name just now. (Aloud, absently, to CAPTAIN THICKNESSE.) No, did you really? How amusing it must have been!

CAPTAIN THICKNESSE - (aggrieved) If you'd done me the honour of payin' any attention to what I was sayin', you'd have found out it wasn't amusin'.

LADY MAISIE - (starting). Oh, wasn't it? I'm so sorry I missed it. I—I'm afraid I was thinking of something else. Do tell me again!

CAPTAIN THICKNESSE - (still hurt). No, I won't inflict it on you—not worth repeatin'. And I should only be takin' off your attention from a fellow that does know how to talk.

LADY MAISIE - (with a guiltiness which she tries to carry off under dignity). I don't think I understand what you mean.

CAPTAIN THICKNESSE - Well, I couldn't help hearin' what you said to your poet-friend before we went in about having to put up with partners; and it isn't what you may call flattering to a fellow's feelin's, being put up with.

LADY MAISIE - (hotly). It—it was not intended for you. You entirely misunderstood!

CAPTAIN THICKNESSE - Dare say I'm very dense; but, even to my comprehension, it's plain enough that the reason why you weren't listenin' to me just now was that the poet had the luck to say somethin' that you found more interesting.

LADY MAISIE - You are quite wrong—it's too absurd; I never even met Mr. Spurrell in my life till this afternoon. If you really must know, I heard him mention my name, and—and I wondered, naturally, what he could possibly be saying.

CAPTAIN THICKNESSE - Somethin' very charmin', and poetical, and complimentary, I'm sure, and I'm makin' you lose it all. Apologise—shan't happen again.

LADY MAISIE - Please be sensible, and let us talk of something else. Are you staying here long?

CAPTAIN THICKNESSE - You will be gratified to hear I leave for Aldershot to-morrow. Meant to have gone to-day. Sorry I didn't now.

LADY MAISIE - I think it was a thousand pities you didn't, as you seem to have stayed on purpose to be as stupid and unkind as you possibly can.

[She turns to her other neighbour, LORD LULLINGTON.

MRS CHATTERIS - (to Captain THICKNESSE, who is on her other side). Oh, Captain Thicknesse, what do you think Mr. Spurrell has just told me? You remember those lines to Lady Grisoline that Mr. Pilliner made such fun of this morning? Well, they were meant for Lady Maisie! They're quite old friends, it seems. So romantic! Wouldn't you like to know how they came to meet?

CAPTAIN THICKNESSE - Can't say I'm particularly curious—no affair of mine, don't you know. (To himself.) And she told me they'd never met before! Sooner I get back the better. Only in the way here.

LADY MAISIE - (turning to him). Well, are you as determined to be as disagreeable as ever? Oh yes, I see you are!

CAPTAIN THICKNESSE - I'm hurt, that's what it is, and I'm not clever at hiding my feelin's. Fact is, I've just been told somethin' that—well, it's no business of mine, only you might have been a little more frank with an old friend, instead of leavin' it to come through somebody else. These things always come out, you know.

LADY MAISIE - (to herself). That wretch has been talking! I knew he would! (Aloud.) I—I know I've been very foolish. If I was to tell you some time—

CAPTAIN THICKNESSE - (hastily). Oh, no reason why you should tell me anything. Assure you, I—I'm not curious.

LADY MAISIE - In that case I shall certainly not trouble you. (To herself.) He may think just what he pleases, I don't care. But, oh, if Mr. Spurrell dares to speak to me after this, I shall astonish him!

LADY RHONDA - (to SPURRELL). I say—I am in a funk. Only just heard who I'm next to. I always do feel such a perfect fool when I've got to talk to a famous person—and you're frightfully famous, aren't you?

SPURRELL - (modestly). Oh, I don't know—I suppose I am, in a sort of way, through Andromeda. Seem to think so here, anyhow.

LADY RHONDA - Well, I'd better tell you at once, I'm no good at poetry—can't make head or tail of it, some'ow. It does seem to me such—well, such footle. Awf'ly rude of me sayin' things like that!

SPURRELL - Is it? I'm just the same—wouldn't give a penny a yard for poetry, myself!

LADY RHONDA - You wouldn't? I am glad. Such a let-off for me! I was afraid you'd want to talk of nothin' else, and the only things I can really talk about are horses and dogs, and that kind of thing.

SPURRELL - That's all right, then. All I don't know about dogs and horses you could put in a homoeopathic globule—and then it would rattle!

LADY RHONDA - Then you're just the man. Look here, I've an Airedale at home, and he's losin' all his coat and—

[They converse with animation.

SPURRELL - (later—to himself). I am getting on. I always knew I was made for Society. If only this coat was easier under the arms!

THOMAS - (behind him—in a discreet whisper). Beg your pardon, sir, but I was requested to 'and you this note, and wait for an answer.

SPURRELL - (opening it, and reading). "Mr. Galfrid Undershell thinks that the gentleman who is occupying the Verney Chamber has, doubtless by inadvertence, put on Mr. Undershell's evening clothes. As he requires them immediately, he will be obliged by an early appointment being made, with a view to their return." (To himself.) Oh, Lor! Then it wasn't Sir Rupert, after all! Just when I was beginning to enjoy my evening, too. What on earth am I to say to this chap? I can't take 'em all off here!

[He sits staring at the paper in blank dismay.

## PART XI

TIME AND THE HOUR

In the Dining-hall.

SPURRELL - (to himself, uncomfortably conscious of the expectant THOMAS in his rear). Must write something to this beggar, I suppose; it'll keep him quiet. (To MRS BROOKE-CHATTERIS.) I—I just want to write a line or two. Could you oblige me with a lead pencil?

MRS CHATTERIS - You are really going to write! At a dinner-party, of all places! Now how delightfully original and unconventional of you! I promise not to interrupt till the inspiration is over. Only, really, I'm afraid I don't carry lead pencils about with me—so bad for one's frocks, you know!

THOMAS - (in his ear). I can lend you a pencil, sir, if you require one.

[He provides him with a very minute stump.

SPURRELL - (reading what he has written on the back of UNDERSHELL'S missive). "Will be in my room (Verney Chamber) as soon after ten as possible.

"J. SPURRELL."

(He passes the paper to THOMAS surreptitiously.) There, take him that.

[THOMAS retires.

ARCHIE BEARPARK - (to himself.) The calm cheek of these writin' chaps! I saw him takin' notes under the table! LADY RHONDA ought to know the sort of fellow he is—and she shall! (To LADY RHONDA, in an aggrieved undertone.) I should advise you to be jolly careful what you say to your other neighbour; he's takin' it all down. I just caught him writin'. He'll be bringing out a satire, or whatever he calls it, on us all by and bye—you see if he won't!

LADY RHONDA - What an ill-natured boy you are! Just because he can write, and you can't. And I don't believe he's doing anythin' of the sort. I'll ask him—I don't care! (Aloud, to SPURRELL.) I say, I know I'm awfully inquisitive—but I do want to know so—you've just been writin' notes or somethin', haven't you? Mr. Bearpark declares you're goin' to take them all off here—you're not really, are you?

SPURRELL - (to himself). That sulky young chap has spotted it! (Aloud, stammering.) I—take everything off? Here! I—I assure you I should never even think of doing anything so indelicate!

LADY RHONDA - I was sure that was what you'd say! But still (with reviving uneasiness), I suppose you have made use of things that happened just to fit your purpose, haven't you?

SPURRELL - (penitently). All I can say is, that—if I have—you won't catch me doing it again! And other people's things don't fit. I'd much rather have my own.

LADY RHONDA - (relieved). Of course! But I'm glad you told me. (To ARCHIE, in an undertone.) I asked him—and, as usual, you were utterly wrong. So you'll please not to be a pig!

ARCHIE BEARPARK - (jealously). And you're goin' to go on talkin' to him all through dinner? Pleasant for me—when I took you down!

LADY RHONDA - You want to be taken down yourself, I think. And I mean to talk to him if I choose. You can talk to Lady Culverin—she likes boys! (Turning to SPURRELL.) I was goin' to ask you—ought a schipperke to have meat? Mine won't touch puppy biscuits.

[SPURRELL enlightens her on this point; ARCHIE glowers.

LADY CANTIRE - (perceiving that the Bishop is showing signs of restiveness). Well, Bishop, I wish I could find you a little more ready to listen to what the other side has to say!

THE BISHOP - (who has been "heckled" to the verge of his endurance.) I am—ah—not conscious of any unreadiness to enter into conversation with the very estimable lady on my other side, should an opportunity present itself.

LADY CANTIRE - Now, that's one of your quibbles, my dear Bishop, and I detest quibbling! But at least it shows you haven't a leg to stand upon.

THE BISHOP - Precisely—nor to—ah—run away upon, dear lady. I am wholly at your mercy, you perceive!

LADY CANTIRE - (triumphantly). Then you admit you're beaten? Oh, I don't despair of you yet, Bishop.

THE BISHOP - I confess I am less sanguine. (To himself.) Shall I have strength to bear these buffets with any remains of Christian forbearance through three more courses? Ha, thank Heaven, the salad!

[He cheers up at the sight of this olive-branch.

MRS EARWAKER - (to PILLINER) Now, I don't altogether approve of the New Woman myself; but still, I am glad to see how women are beginning to assert themselves and come to the front; surely you sympathise with all that?

PILLINER - (plaintively). No, really I can't, you know! I'd so much rather they wouldn't. They've made us poor men feel positively obsolete! They'll snub us out of existence soon—our sex will be extinct—and then they'll be sorry. There'll be nobody to protect them from one another! After all, we can't help being what we are. It isn't my fault that I was born a Man Thing—now, is it?

LADY CANTIRE - (overhearing this remark). Well, if it is a fault, Mr. Pilliner, we must all acknowledge that you've done everything in your power to correct it!

PILLINER - (sweetly). How nice and encouraging of you, dear Lady Cantire, to take up the cudgels for me like that!

[LADY CANTIRE privately relieves her feelings by expressing a preference for taking up a birch rod, and renews her attack on the Bishop.

MR SHOPRTHORN - (who has been dragging his mental depths for a fresh topic—hopefully, to MISS SPELWANE). By the bye, I haven't asked you what you thought about these—er—revolting daughters?

MISS SPELWANE - No, you haven't; and I thought it so considerate of you.

[Mr. SHORTHORN gives up dragging, in discouragement.

PILLINER - (sotto voce, to MISS SPELWANE). Have you quite done sitting on that poor unfortunate man? I heard you!

MISS SPELWANE - (in the same tone). I'm afraid I have been rather beastly to him. But, oh, he is such a bore—he would talk about his horrid "silos," till I asked him whether they would eat out of his hand. After that, the subject dropped—somehow.

PILLINER - I see you've been punishing him for not happening to be a distinguished poet. I thought he was to have been the fortunate man?

MISS SPELWANE - So he was; but they changed it all at the last moment; it really was rather provoking. I could have talked to him.

PILLINER — Lady Rhonda appears to be consoling him. Poor dear old Archie's face is quite a study. But really I don't see that his poetry is so very wonderful; no more did you this morning!

MISS SPELWANE - Because you deliberately picked out the worst bits, and read them as badly as you could!

PILLINER - Ah, well, he's here to read them for himself now. I dare say he'd be delighted to be asked.

MISS SPELWANE - Do you know, Bertie, that's rather a good idea of yours. I'll ask him to read us something to-night.

PILLINER - (aghast). To-night! With all these people here? I say, they'll never stand it, you know.

[LADY CULVERIN gives the signal.

MISS SPELWANE - (as she rises). They ought to feel it an immense privilege. I know I shall.

THE BISHOP - (to himself, as he rises). Port in sight—at last! But, oh, what I have had to suffer!

LADY CANTIRE - (at parting). Well, we've had quite one of our old discussions. I always enjoy talking to you, Bishop. But I haven't yet got at your reasons for voting as you did on the Parish Councils Bill; we must go into that upstairs.

THE BISHOP - (with strict veracity). I shall be—ah—all impatience, Lady Cantire (To himself.) I fervently trust that a repetition of this experience may yet be spared me!

LADY RHONDA - (as she leaves SPURRELL). You will tell me the name of the stuff upstairs, won't you? So very much ta!

ARCHIE BEARPARK - (to himself). I'd like to tar him very much, and feather him too, for cuttin' me out like this! (The men sit down; SPURRELL finds himself between ARCHIE and CAPTAIN THICKNESSE, at the further end of the table; ARCHIE passes the wine to SPURRELL with a scowl.) What are you drinkin'? Claret? What do you do your writin' on, now, as a general thing?

SPURRELL - (on the defensive). On paper, sir, when I've any to do. Do you do yours on a slate?

CAPTAIN THICKNESSE - I say, that's rather good. Had you there, Bearpark!

SPURRELL - (to ARCHIE, lowering his voice). Look here, I see you're trying to put a spoke in my wheel. You saw me writing at dinner, and went and told that young lady I was going to take everything off there and then, which you must have known I wasn't likely to do. Now, sir, it's no business of yours that I can see; but, as you seem to be interested, I may tell you that I shall go up and do it in my own room, as soon as I leave this table, and there will be no fuss or publicity about it whatever. I hope you're satisfied now?

ARCHIE BEARPARK - Oh, I'm satisfied. (He rises.) Left my cigarette-case upstairs—horrid bore—must go and get it.

CAPTAIN THICKNESSE - They'll be bringing some round in another minute.

ARCHIE BEARPARK - Prefer my own. (To himself, as he leaves the hall.) I knew I was right. That bounder is meaning to scribble some rot about us all! He's goin' straight up to his room to do it.... Well, he may find a little surprise when he gets there!

CAPTAIN THICKNESSE - (to himself). Mustn't let this poet fellow think I'm jealous; dare say, after all, there's nothing serious between them. Not that it matters to me; any way, I may as well talk to him. I wonder if he knows anything about steeplechasin'.

[He discovers that SPURRELL is not unacquainted with this branch of knowledge.

In a Corridor leading to the Housekeeper's Room.

TIME—9.30 P.M.

UNDERSHELL - (to himself). If I wasn't absolutely compelled by sheer hunger, I would not touch a morsel in this house. But I can't get my things back till after ten. As soon as ever I do, I will insist on a conveyance to the nearest inn. In the meantime I must sup. After all, no one need know of this humiliating adventure. And if I am compelled to consort with these pampered menials, I think I shall know how to preserve my dignity—even while adapting myself to their level. And that girl will be there—a distinctly redeeming fact in the situation. I will be easy—affable, even; I will lay aside all foolish pride; it would be unreasonable to visit their employer's snobbery upon their unoffending heads. I hear conversation inside this room. This must be the door. I—I suppose I had better go in.

[He enters.

## PART XII

DIGNITY UNDER DIFFICULTIES

In the Housekeeper's Room at Wyvern; MRS POMFRET, the Housekeeper, in a black silk gown and her smartest cap, is seated in a winged armchair by the fire, discussing domestic politics with LADY CULVERIN'S maid, MISS STICKLER. The Chef, M. RIDEVOS, is resting on the sofa, in languid converse with Mlle. CHIFFON, MISS SPELWANE'S maid; PILLINER'S man, LOUCH, watches STEPTOE, SIR RUPERT'S valet, with admiring envy, as he makes himself agreeable to Miss PHILLIPSON, who is in demi-toilette, as are all the other ladies' maids present.

MISS STICKLER - (in an impressive undertone). All I do say, Mrs. Pomfret, ma'am, is this: if that girl Louisa marches into the pew to-morrow, as she did last Sunday, before the second laundry maid—and her only under-scullery maid—such presumptiousness should be put a stop to in future!

MRS POMFRET - (wheezily). Depend upon it, my dear, it's her ignorance; but I shall most certainly speak about it. Girls must be taught that ranks was made to be respected, and the precedency into that pew has come down from time immemoriable, and is not to be set aside by such as her while I'm 'ousekeeper here.

Mlle. CHIFFON - (in French, to M. RIDEVOS). You have the air fatigued, my poor friend! Oh, there—but fatigued!

M. RIDEVOS - (Broken, Mademoiselle, absolutely broken. But what will you? This night I surpass myself. I achieve a masterpiece—a sublime pyramid of quails with a sauce that will become classic. I pay now the penalty of a veritable crisis of nerves. It is of my temperament as artist.

Mlle. CHIFFON - And me, my poor friend, how I have suffered from the cookery of these others—I who have the stomach so feeble, so fastidious! Figure to yourself an existence upon the villainous curry, the abominable "Iahristue," beloved by these barbarians, but which succeed with me not at all—oh, but not at all! Since I am here—ah, the difference! I digest as of old—I am gay. But next week to return with mademoiselle to the curry, my poor friend, what regrets!

M. RIDEVOS - (For me, dear mademoiselle, for me the regrets—to hear no more the conversation, so spiritual, so sympathetic, of a fellow-countrywoman. For remark that here they are stupid—they comprehend not. And the old ones they roll at me the eyes to make terror. Behold this Gorgon who approaches. She adores me, my word of honour, this ruin!

[Miss STICKLER comes up to the sofa smiling in happy unconsciousness.

MISS STICKLER - (graciously). So you've felt equal to joining us for once, Mossoo! We feel it a very 'igh compliment, I can assure you. We've really been feeling quite 'urt at the way you keep to yourself—you might be a regular 'ermit for all we see of you!

M. RIDEVOS - (For invent, dear Mees, for create, ze arteeste must live ze solitaire as of rule. To-night—no! I emairge, as you see, to res-tore myself viz your smile.

MISS STICKLER - (flattered). Well, I've always said, Mossoo, and I always will say, that for polite 'abits and pretty speeches, give me a Frenchman!

M. RIDEVOS - (alarmed). For me it is too moch 'appiness. For anozzer, ah!

[He kisses his fingers with ineffable grace.

PHILLIPSON - (advancing to meet MISS DOLMAN, who has just entered). Why, I'd no idea I should meet you here, Sarah! And how have you been getting on, dear? Still with—?

MISS DOLMAN - (checking her with a look). Her grace? No, we parted some time ago. I'm with Lady Rhonda Cokayne at present. (In an undertone, as she takes her aside.) You needn't say anything here of your having known me at Mrs. Dickenson's. I couldn't afford to have it get about in the circle I'm in that I'd ever lived with any but the nobility. I'm sure you see what I mean. Of course I don't mind your saying we've met.

PHILLIPSON - Oh, I quite understand. I'll say nothing. I'm obliged to be careful myself, being maid to Lady Maisie Mull.

MISS DOLMAN - My dear Emma! It is nice seeing you again—such friends as we used to be!

PHILLIPSON - At her Grace's? I'm afraid you're thinking of somebody else. (She crosses to MRS POMFRET.) Mrs. Pomfret, what's become of the gentleman I travelled down with—the horse doctor? I do hope he means to come in; he would amuse you, Mr. Steptoe. I never heard anybody go on like him; he did make me laugh so!

MRS POMFRET - I really can't say where he is, my dear. I sent up word to let him know he was welcome here whenever he pleased; but perhaps he's feeling a little shy about coming down.

PHILLIPSON - Oh, I don't think he suffers much from that. (As the door opens.) Ah, there he is!

MRS POMFRET - (rising, with dignity, to receive UNDERSHELL, who enters in obvious embarrassment). Come in, sir. I'm glad to see you've found your way down at last. Let me see, I haven't the advantage of knowing your—Mr. Undershell, to be sure! Well, Mr. Undershell, we're very pleased to see you. I hope you'll make yourself quite at home. Her ladyship gave particular directions that we was to look after you—most particular she was!

UNDERSHELL - You are very good, ma'am. I am obliged to Lady Culverin for her (with a gulp) condescension. But I shall not trespass more than a short time upon your hospitality.

MRS POMFRET - Don't speak of it as trespassing, sir. It's not often we have a gentleman of your profession as a visitor, but you are none the less welcome. Now I'd better introduce you all round, and then you won't feel yourself a stranger. Miss Phillipson you have met, I know.

[She introduces him to the others in turn; UNDERSHELL bows helplessly.

STEPTOE - (with urbanity). Your fame, sir, has preceded you. And you'll find us a very friendly and congenial little circle on a better acquaintance—if this is your first experience of this particular form of society?

UNDERSHELL - (to himself). I mustn't be stiff, I'll put them at their ease. (Aloud.) Why, I must admit, Mr. Steptoe, that I have never before had the privilege of entering the—(with an ingratiating smile all round him) the "Pugs' Parlour," as I understand you call this very charming room.

[The company draw themselves up and cough in disapprobation.

STEPTOE - (very stiffly). Pardon me, sir, you have been totally misinformed. Such an expression is not current here.

MRS POMFRET - (more stiffly still). It is never alluded to in my presence except as the 'ousekeeper's room, which is the right and proper name for it. There may be some other term for it in the servants' 'all for anything I know to the contrary—but, if you'll excuse me for saying so, Mr. Undershell, we'd prefer for it not to be repeated in our presence.

UNDERSHELL - (confusedly). I—I beg ten thousand pardons. (To himself.) To be pulled up like this for trying to be genial—it's really too humiliating!

STEPTOE - (relaxing). Well, well, sir; we must make some allowances for a neophyte. You'll know better another time, I dare say. Miss Phillipson here has been giving you a very favourable character as a highly agreeable rattle, Mr. Undershell. I hope we may be favoured with a specimen of your social talents later on. We're always grateful here for anything in that way—such as a recitation now, or a comic song, or a yumorous imitation—anything, in short, calculated to promote the general harmony and festivity will be appreciated.

MISS STICKLER - (acidly). Provided it is free from any helement of coarseness, which we do not encourage—far from it!

UNDERSHELL - (suppressing his irritation). You need be under no alarm, madam. I do not propose to attempt a performance of any kind.

PHILLIPSON - Don't be so solemn, Mr. Undershell! I'm sure you can be as comical as any play-actor when you choose!

UNDERSHELL - I really don't know how I can have given you that impression. If you expect me to treat my lyre like a horse-collar, and grin through it, I'm afraid I am unable to gratify you.

STEPTOE - (at sea). Capital, sir, the professional allusion very neat. You'll come out presently, I can see, when supper's on the table. Can't expect you to rattle till you've something inside of you, can we?

MISS STICKLET - Reelly, Mr. Steptoe, I am surprised at such commonness from you!

STEPTOE - Now you're too severe, Miss Stickler, you are indeed. An innocent little Judy Mow like that!

TREDWELL - (outside). Don't answer me, sir. Ham I butler 'ere, or ham I not? I've a precious good mind to report you for such a hignorant blunder.... I don't want to hear another word about the gentleman's cloes—you'd no hearthly business for to do such a thing at all! (He enters and flings himself down on a chair.) That Thomas is beyond everything—stoopid hass as he is!

MRS POMFRET - (concerned). La, Mr. Tredwell, you do seem put out! Whatever have Thomas been doing now?

UNDERSHELL - (to himself). It's really very good of him to take it to heart like this! (Aloud.) Pray don't let it distress you; it's of no consequence, none at all!

TREDWELL - (glaring). I'm the best judge of that, Mr. Undershell, sir—if you'll allow me; I don't call my porogatives of no consequence, whatever you may! And that feller Thomas, Mrs. Pomfret, actially 'ad the hordacity, without consulting me previous, to go and 'and a note to one of our gentlemen at the hupstairs table, all about some hassinine mistake he'd made with his cloes! What call had he to take it upon himself? I feel puffecly disgraced that such a thing should have occurred under my authority!

[THE STEWARD'S ROOM BOY has entered with a dish, and listens with secret anxiety on his own account.

UNDERSHELL - I assure you there is no harm done. The gentleman is wearing my evening clothes—but he's going to return them—

[The conclusion of the sentence is drowned in a roar of laughter from the majority.

TREDWELL - (gasping). Hevenin' cloes! Your hevenin'— P'raps you'll 'ave the goodness to explain yourself, sir!

STEPTOE - No, no, Tredwell, my dear fellah, you don't understand our friend here—he's a bit of a wag, don't you see? He's only trying to pull your leg, that's all; and, Gad, he did it too! But you mustn't take liberties with this gentleman, Mr. Undershell; he's an important personage here, I can tell you!

UNDERSHELL - (earnestly). But I never meant—if you'll only let me explain—

[The STEWARD'S ROOM BOY has come behind him, and administers a surreptitious kick, which UNDERSHELL rightly construes as a hint to hold his tongue.

TREDWELL - (in solemn offence). I'm accustomed, Mr. Hundershell, to be treated in this room with respect and deference—especially by them as come here in the capacity of guests. From such I regard any attempt to pull my leg as in hindifferent taste—to say the least of it. I wish to 'ave no more words on the subjick, which is a painful one, and had better be dropped, for the sake of all parties. Mrs. Pomfret, I see supper is on the table, so, by your leave, we had better set down to it.

PHILLIPSON - (to UNDERSHELL). Never mind him, pompous old thing! It was awfully cheeky of you, though. You can sit next me if you like.

UNDERSHELL - (to himself, as he avails himself of this permission). I shall only make things worse if I explain now. But, oh, great Heavens, what a position for a poet!

## PART XIII

WHAT'S IN A NAME?

At the Supper-table in the Housekeeper's Room. MRS POMFRET and TREDWELL are at the head and foot of the table respectively. UNDERSHELL is between MRS POMFRET and MISS PHILLIPSON. THE STEWARD'S ROOM BOY waits.

TREDWELL - I don't see Mr. Adams here this evening, Mrs. Pomfret. What's the reason of that?

Mrs. Pomfret. Why, he asked to be excused to-night, Mr. Tredwell. You see some of the visitors' coachmen are putting up their horses here, and he's helping Mr. Checkley entertain them. (To UNDERSHELL.) Mr. Adams is our stud-groom, and him and Mr. Checkley, the 'ed coachman, are very friendly just now. Adams is very clever with his horses, I believe, and I'm sure he'd have liked a talk with you; it's a pity he's engaged elsewhere this evening.

UNDERSHELL - (mystified). I—I'm exceedingly sorry to have missed him, ma'am. (To himself.) Is the stud-groom literary, I wonder?... Ah, no, I remember now; I allowed Miss Phillipson to conclude that my tastes were equestrian. Perhaps it's just as well the stud-groom isn't here!

MRS POMFRET - Well, he may drop in later on. I shouldn't be surprised if you and he had met before.

UNDERSHELL - (to himself). I should. (Aloud.) I hardly think it's probable.

MRS POMFRET - I've known stranger things than that happen. Why, only the other day, a gentleman came into this very room, as it might be yourself, and it struck me he was looking very hard at me, and by and bye he says, "You don't recollect me, ma'am, but I know you very well," says he. So I said to him, "You certainly have the advantage of me at present, sir." "Well, ma'am," he says, "many years ago I had the honour and privilege of being steward's room boy in a house where you was still-room maid; and I consider I owe the position I have since attained entirely to the good advice you used to give me, as I've never forgot it, ma'am," says he. Then it flashed across me who it was—"Mr. Pocklington!" says I. Which it were. And him own man to the Duke of Dumbleshire! Which was what made it so very nice and 'andsome of him to remember me all that time.

UNDERSHELL - (perfunctorily). It must have been most gratifying, ma'am. (To himself.) I hope this old lady hasn't any more anecdotes of this highly interesting nature. I mustn't neglect Miss Phillipson—especially as I haven't very long to stay here.

[He consults his watch stealthily.

Miss PHILLIPSON - (observing the action). I'm sorry you find it so slow here; it's not very polite of you to show it quite so openly though, I must say.

[She pouts.

UNDERSHELL - (to himself). I can't let this poor girl think me a brute! But I must be careful not to go too far. (To her, in an undertone which he tries to render unemotional.) Don't misunderstand me like that. If I looked at my watch, it was merely to count the minutes that are left. In one short half-hour I must go—I must pass out of your life, and you must forget—oh, it will be easy for you—but for me, ah! you cannot think that I shall carry away a heart entirely unscathed! Believe me, I shall always look back gratefully, regretfully, on—

PHILLIPSON - (bending her head with a gratified little giggle). I declare you're beginning all that again. I never did see such a cure as you are.

UNDERSHELL - (to himself, displeased). I wish she could bring herself to take me a little more seriously. I can not consider it a compliment to be called a "cure"—whatever that is.

STEPTOE - (considering it time to interfere). Come, Mr. Undershell, all this whispering reelly is not fair on the company! You mustn't hide your bushel under a napkin like this; don't reserve all your sparklers for Miss Phillipson there.

UNDERSHELL - (stiffly). I—ah—was not making any remark that could be described as a sparkler, sir. I don't sparkle.

PHILLIPSON - (demurely). He was being rather sentimental just then, Mr. Steptoe, as it happens. Not that he can't sparkle, when he likes. I'm sure if you'd heard how he went on in the fly!

STEPTOE - (with malice). Not having been privileged to be present, perhaps our friend here could recollect a few of his happiest efforts and repeat them.

MISS DOLMAN - Do, Mr. Undershell, please. I do love a good laugh.

UNDERSHELL - (crimson). I—you really must excuse me. I said nothing worth repeating. I don't remember that I was particularly—

STEPTOE - Pardon me. Afraid I was indiscreet. We must spare Miss Phillipson's blushes by all manner of means.

PHILLIPSON - Oh, it was nothing of that sort, Mr. Steptoe! I've no objection to repeat what he said. He called me a little green something or other. No; he said that in the train, though. But he would have it that the old cab-horse was a magic steed, and the fly an enchanted chariot; and I don't know what all. (As nobody smiles.) It sounded awfully funny as he said it, with his face perfectly solemn like it is now, I assure you it did!

STEPTOE - (patronisingly). I can readily believe it. We shall have you contributing to some of our yumerous periodicals, Mr. Undershell, sir, before long. Such facetious talent is too good to be lost, it reelly is.

UNDERSHELL - (to himself, writhing). I gave her credit for more sense. To make me publicly ridiculous like this!

[He sulks.

MISS STICKLER - (to M. RIDEVOS, who suddenly rises). Mossoo, you're not going! Why, whatever's the matter?

M. RIDEVOS - (Pairmeet zat I make my depart. I am cot at ze art.

[General outcry and sensation.

MRS POMFRET - (concerned). You never mean that, Mossoo? And a nice dish of quails just put on, too, that they haven't even touched upstairs!

M. RIDEVOS - (It is for zat I do not remmain! Zey 'ave not toch him; my pyramide, result of a genius stupend, énorme! to zem he is nossing; zey retturn him to crash me! To-morrow I demmand zat miladi accept my demission. Ici je souffre trop!

[He leaves the room precipitately.

MISS STICKLER - (offering to rise). It does seem to have upset him! Shall I go after him and see if I can't bring him round?

MRS POMFRET - (severely). Stay where you are, Harriet; he's better left to himself. If he wasn't so wropped up in his cookery, he'd know there's always a dish as goes the round untasted, without why or wherefore. I've no patience with the man!

TREDWELL - (philosophically). That's the worst of 'aving to do with Frenchmen; they're so apt to beyave with a sutting childishness that—(checking himself)—I really ask your pardon, mamsell, I quite forgot you was of his nationality; though it ain't to be wondered at, I'm sure, for you might pass for an Englishwoman almost anywhere!

Mlle. CHIFFON - As you for Frenchman, hein?

TREDWELL - No, 'ang it all, mamsell, I 'ope there's no danger o' that! (To MISS PHILLIPSON.) Delighted to see the Countess keeps as fit as ever, Miss Phillipson! Wonderful woman for her time o' life! Law, she did give the Bishop beans at dinner, and no mistake!

PHILLIPSON - Her ladyship is pretty generous with them to most people, Mr. Tredwell. I'm sure I'd have left her long ago, if it wasn't for Lady Maisie—who is a lady, if you like!

TREDWELL - She don't favour her ma, I will say that for her. By the way, who is the party they brought down with them? a youngish looking chap—seemed a bit out of his helement, when he first come in, though he's soon got over that, judging by the way him and your LADY RHONDA, Miss Dolman, was 'obnobbing together at table!

PHILLIPSON - Nobody came down with my ladies; they must have met him in the bus, I expect. What is his name?

TREDWELL - Why, he give it to me, I know, when I enounced him; but it's gone clean out of my head again. He's got the Verney Chamber, I know that much; but what was his name again? I shall forget my own next.

UNDERSHELL - (involuntarily). In the Verney Chamber? Then the name must be Spurrell!

PHILLIPSON - (starting). Spurrell! Why, I used to— But of course it can't be him!

TREDWELL - Spurrell was the name, though. (With a resentful glare at UNDERSHELL.) I don't know how you came to be aware of it, sir!

UNDERSHELL - Why, the fact is, I happened to find out that—(here he receives an admonitory drive in the back from the Boy)—that his name was Spurrell. (To himself.) I wish this infernal boy wouldn't be officious—but perhaps he's right!

TREDWELL - Ho, indeed! Well, another time, Mr. Hundershell, if you require information about parties staying with us, p'raps you'll be good enough to apply to me pussonally, instead of picking it up in some 'ole-and-corner fashion. (UNDERSHELL controls his indignation with difficulty.) To return to the individual in question, Miss Phillipson, I should have said myself he was something in the artistic or littery way; he suttingly didn't give me the impression of being a gentleman.

PHILLIPSON - (to herself, relieved). Then it isn't my Jem! I might have known he wouldn't be visiting here, and carrying on with Lady Rhonda. He'd never forget himself like that—if he has forgotten me!

STEPTOE - It strikes me he's more of a sporting character, Tredwell. I know when I was circulating with the cigarettes and so on, in the hall just now, he was telling the Captain some anecdote about an old steeplechaser that was faked up to win a selling handicap, and it tickled me to that extent I could hardly hold the spirit-lamp steady.

TREDWELL - I may be mistook, Steptoe. All I can say is, that when me and James was serving cawfy to the ladies in the drawing-room, some of them had got 'old of a little pink book all sprinkled over with silver cutlets, and, rightly or wrongly, I took it to 'ave some connection with 'im.

UNDERSHELL - (excitedly). Pink and silver! Might I ask—was it a volume of poetry, called—er—Andromeda?

TREDWELL - (crushingly). That I did not take the liberty of inquiring, sir, as you might be aware if you was a little more familiar with the hetiquette of good society.

[UNDERSHELL collapses; MR ADAMS enters, and steps into the chair vacated by the Chef, next to MRS POMFRET, with whom he converses.

UNDERSHELL - (to himself). To think that they may be discussing my book in the drawing-room at this very moment, while I—I— (He chokes.) Ah, it won't bear thinking of! I must—I will get out of this accursed place! I have stood this too long as it is! But I won't go till I have seen this fellow Spurrell, and made him give me back my things. What's the time? ... ten! I can go at last. (He rises.) Mrs. Pomfret, will you kindly excuse me? I—I find I must go at once.

MRS POMFRET - Well, Mr. Undershell, sir, you're the best judge; and, if you really can't stop, this is Mr. Adams, who'll take you round to the stables himself, and do anything that's necessary. Won't you, Mr. Adams?

ADAMS - So you're off to-night, sir, are you? Well, I'd rather ha' shown you Deerfoot by daylight, myself; but there, I dessay that won't make much difference to you, so long as you do see the 'orse?

UNDERSHELL - (to himself). So Deerfoot's a horse! One of the features of Wyvern, I suppose; they seem very anxious I shouldn't miss it. I don't want to see the beast; but I dare say it won't take many minutes; and, if I don't humour this man, I shan't get a conveyance to go away in! (Aloud.) No difference whatever—to me. I shall be delighted to be shown Deerfoot; only I really can't wait much longer; I—I've an appointment elsewhere!

ADAMS - Right, sir; you get your 'at and coat, and come along with me, and you shall see him at once.

[UNDERSHELL takes a hasty farewell of MISS PHILLIPSON and the company generally—none of whom attempts to detain him—and follows his guide. As the door closes upon them, he hears a burst of stifled merriment, amidst which MISS PHILLIPSON'S laughter is only too painfully recognisable.

PART XIV

LE VÉTÉRINAIRE MALGRÉ LUI

Outside the Stables at Wyvern.

TIME—About 10 P.M.

UNDERSHELL - (to himself, as he follows ADAMS). Now is my time to arrange about getting away from here. (To ADAMS.) By the bye, I suppose you can let me have a conveyance of some sort—after I've seen the horse? I—I'm rather in a hurry.

ADAMS - You'd better speak to Mr. Checkley about that, sir; it ain't in my department, you see. I'll fetch him round, if you'll wait here a minute; he'd like to hear what you think about the 'orse.

[He goes off to the coachman's quarters.

UNDERSHELL - (alone). A very civil fellow this; he seems quite anxious to show me this animal! There must be something very remarkable about it.

[ADAMS returns with CHECKLEY.

ADAMS - Mr. Checkley, our 'ed coachman, Mr. Undershell. He's coming in along with us to 'ear what you say, if you've no objections.

UNDERSHELL - (to himself). I must make a friend of this coachman, or else— (Aloud.) I shall be charmed, Mr. CHECKLEY - I've only a very few minutes to spare; but I'm most curious to see this horse of yours.

CHECKLEY - He ain't one o' my 'orses, sir. If he 'ad been— But there, I'd better say nothing about it.

ADAMS - (as he leads the way into the stables, and turns up the gas). There, sir, that's Deerfoot over there in the loose box.

UNDERSHELL - (to himself). He seems to me much like any other horse! However, I can't be wrong in admiring. (Aloud, as he inspects him, through the rails.) Ah, indeed? he is worth seeing! A magnificent creature!

ADAMS - (stripping off Deerfoot's clothing). He's a good 'orse, sir. Her ladyship won't trust herself on no other animal, not since she 'ad the influenzy so bad. She'd take on dreadful if I 'ad to tell her he wouldn't be fit for no more work, she would!

UNDERSHELL - (sympathetically). I can quite imagine so. Not that he seems in any danger of that!

CHECKLEY - (triumphantly). There, you 'ear that, Adams? The minute he set eyes on the 'orse!

ADAMS - Wait till Mr. Undershell has seen him move a bit, and see what he says then.

CHECKLEY - If it was what you think, he'd never be standing like he is now, depend upon it.

ADAMS - You can't depend upon it. He 'eard us coming, and he's quite artful enough to draw his foot back for fear o' getting a knock. (To UNDERSHELL.) I've noticed him very fidgety-like on his forelegs this last day or two.

UNDERSHELL - Have you, though? (To himself.) I hope he won't be fidgety with his hind-legs. I shall stay outside.

ADAMS - I cooled him down with a rubub and aloes ball, and kep 'im on low diet; but he don't seem no better.

UNDERSHELL - (to himself). I didn't gather the horse was unwell. (Aloud.) Dear me! no better? You don't say so!

CHECKLEY - If you'd rubbed a little embrocation into the shoulder, you'd ha' done more good, in my opinion, and it's my belief as Mr. Undershell here will tell you I'm right.

UNDERSHELL - (to himself). Can't afford to offend the coachman! (Aloud.) Well, I dare say—er— embrocation would have been better.

ADAMS - Ah, that's where me and Mr. Checkley differ. According to me, it ain't to do with the shoulder at all—it's a deal lower down.... I'll 'ave him out of the box and you'll soon see what I mean.

UNDERSHELL - (hastily). Pray don't trouble on my account. I—I can see him capitally from where I am, thanks.

ADAMS - You know best, sir. Only I thought you'd be better able to form a judgment after you'd seen the way he stepped across. But if you was to come in and examine the frog?— I don't like the look of it myself.

UNDERSHELL - (to himself). I'm sure I don't. I've a horror of reptiles. (Aloud.) You're very good. I—I think I won't come in. The place must be rather damp, mustn't it—for that?

ADAMS - It's dry enough in 'ere, sir, as you may see; nor yet he ain't been standing about in no wet. Still, there it is, you see!

UNDERSHELL - (to himself). What a fool he must be not to drive it out! Of course it must annoy the horse. (Aloud.) I don't see it; but I'm quite willing to take your word for it.

ADAMS - I don't know how you can expect to see it, sir, without you look inside of the 'oof for it.

UNDERSHELL - (to himself). It's not alive—it's something inside the hoof. I suppose I ought to have known that. (Aloud.) Just so; but I see no necessity for looking inside the hoof.

CHECKLEY - In course he don't, or he'd ha' looked the very fust thing, with all his experience. I 'ope you're satisfied now, Adams?

ADAMS - I can't say as I am. I say as no man can examine a 'orse thoroughly at that distance, be he who he may. And whether I'm right or wrong, it 'ud be more of a satisfaction to me if Mr. Undershell was to step in and see the 'oof for himself.

CHECKLEY - Well, there's sense in that, and I dessay Mr. Undershell won't object to obliging you that far.

UNDERSHELL - (with reluctance). Oh, with pleasure, if you make a point of it.

[He enters the loose box delicately.

ADAMS - (picking up one of the horse's feet). Now, tell me how this 'ere 'oof strikes you.

UNDERSHELL - (to himself). That hoof can't; but I'm not so sure about the others. (Aloud, as he inspects it.) Well—er—it seems to me a very nice hoof.

ADAMS - (grimly). I was not arsking your opinion of it as a work of art, sir. Do you see any narrering coming on, or do you not? That's what I should like to get out of you!

UNDERSHELL - (to himself). Does this man suppose I collect hoofs! However, I'm not going to commit myself. (Aloud.) H'm—well, I—I rather agree with Mr. Checkley.

CHECKLEY - I knew he would! Now you've got it, Adams! I can see Mr. Undershell knows what he's about.

ADAMS - (persistently). But look at this 'ere pastern. You can't deny there's puffiness there. How do you get over that?

UNDERSHELL - If the horse is puffy, it's his business to get over it—not mine.

ADAMS - (aggrieved). You may think proper to treat it light, sir; but if you put your 'and down 'ere, above the coronet, you'll feel a throbbing as plain as—

UNDERSHELL - Very likely. But I don't know, really, that it would afford me any particular gratification if I did!

ADAMS - Well, if you don't take my view, I should ha' thought as you'd want to feel the 'orse's pulse.

UNDERSHELL - You are quite mistaken. I don't. (To himself.) Particularly as I shouldn't know where to find it. What a bore this fellow is with his horse!

CHECKLEY - In course, sir, you see what's running in Mr. Adams's 'ed all this time, what he's a-driving at, eh?

UNDERSHELL - (to himself). I only wish I did! This will require tact. (Aloud.) I—I could hardly avoid seeing that—could I?

CHECKLEY - I should think not. And it stands to reason as a vet like yourself'd spot a thing like navickler fust go off.

UNDERSHELL - (to himself). A vet! They've been taking me for a vet all this time! I can't have been so ignorant as I thought. I really don't like to undeceive them—they might feel annoyed. (Aloud, knowingly.) To be sure, I—I spotted it at once.

ADAMS - He does make it out navicular after all! What did I tell you, Checkley? Now p'raps you'll believe me!

CHECKLEY - I'll be shot if that 'orse has navickler, whoever says so—there!

ADAMS - (gloomily). It's the 'orse 'll 'ave to be shot; worse luck! I'd ha' give something if Mr. Undershell could ha' shown I was wrong; but there was very little doubt in my mind what it was all along.

UNDERSHELL - (to himself, horrified). I've been pronouncing this unhappy animal's doom without knowing it! I must tone it down. (Aloud.) No—no, I never said he must be shot. There's no reason to despair. It—it's quite a mild form of er—clavicular—not at all infectious at present. And the horse has a splendid constitution. I—I really think he'll soon be himself again, if we only—er—leave Nature to do her work, you know.

ADAMS - (after a prolonged whistle). Well, if Nature ain't better up in her work than you seem to be, it's 'igh time she chucked it, and took to something else. You've a lot to learn about navicular, you 'ave, if you can talk such rot as that!

CHECKLEY - Ah, I've 'ad to do with a vet or two in my time, but I'm blest if I ever come across the likes o' you afore!

UNDERSHELL - (to himself). I knew they'd find me out! I must pacify them. (Aloud.) But, look here, I'm not a vet. I never said I was. It was your mistake entirely. The fact is, my—my good men, I came down here because—well, it's unnecessary to explain now why I came. But I'm most anxious to get away, and if you, my dear Mr. Checkley, could let me have a trap to take me to Shuntingbridge to-night, I should feel extremely obliged.

[CHECKLEY stares, deprived of speech.

ADAMS - (with a private wink to CHECKLEY). Certainly he will, sir. I'm sure Checkley 'll feel proud to turn out, late as it is, to oblige a gentleman with your remarkable knowledge of 'orseflesh. Drive you over hisself in the broom and pair, I shouldn't wonder!

UNDERSHELL - One horse will be quite sufficient. Very well, then. I'll just run up and get my portmanteau, and—and one or two things of mine, and if you will be round at the back entrance—don't trouble to drive up to the front door—as soon as possible, I won't keep you waiting longer than I can help. Good evening, Mr. Adams, and many thanks. (To himself, as he hurries back to the house.) I've got out of that rather well. Now, I've only to find my way to the Verney Chamber, see this fellow Spurrell, and get my clothes back, and then I can retreat with comfort, and even dignity! These Culverins shall learn that there is at least one poet who will not put up with their insolent patronage!

CHECKLEY - (to ADAMS). He has got a cool cheek, and no mistake! But if he waits to be druv over to Shuntingbridge till I come round for him, he'll 'ave to set on that portmanteau of his a goodish time!

ADAMS - He did you pretty brown, I must say. To 'ear you crowing over me when he was on your side. I could 'ardly keep from larfing!

CHECKLEY - I see he warn't no vet long afore you, but I let it go on for the joke of it. It was rich to see you a-wanting him to feel the 'oof, and give it out navickler. Well, you got his opinion for what it was wuth, so you're all right!

ADAMS - You think nobody knows anything about 'orses but yourself, you do; but if you're meanin' to make a story out o' this against me, why, I shall tell it my way, that's all!

CHECKLEY - It was you he made a fool of, not me—and I can prove it—there!

[They dispute the point, with rising warmth, for some time.

ADAMS - (calming down). Well, see 'ere, Checkley, I dunno, come to think of it, as either on us 'll show up partickler smart over this 'ere job; and it strikes me we'd better both agree to keep quiet about it, eh? (CHECKLEY acquiesces, not unwillingly.) And I think I'll take a look in at the 'ousekeeper's-room presently, and try if I can't drop a hint to old Tredwell about that smooth-tongued chap, for it's my belief he ain't down 'ere for no good!

## PART XV

TRAPPED!

In a Gallery outside the Verney Chamber.

TIME—About 10.15 P.M.

UNDERSHELL - (to himself, as he emerges from a back staircase). I suppose this is the corridor? The boy said the name of the room was painted up over the door.... Ah, there it is; and, yes, Mr. Spurrell's name on a card.... The door is ajar; he is probably waiting for me inside. I shall meet him quite temperately, treat it simply as a— (He enters; a waste-paper basket, containing an ingenious arrangement of liquid and solid substances, descends on his head.) What the devil do you mean, sir, by this outrageous—? All dark! Nobody here! Is there a general conspiracy to insult me? Have I been lured up here for a brutal— (SPURRELL bursts in.) Ah, there you are, sir! (With cold dignity, through the lattice-work of the basket.) Will you kindly explain what this means?

SPURRELL - Wait till I strike a light. (After lighting a pair of candles.) Well, sir, if you don't know why you're ramping about like that under a waste-paper basket, I can hardly be expected to—

UNDERSHELL - I was determined not to remove it until somebody came in; it fell on my head the moment I entered; it contained something in a soap-dish, which has wetted my face. You may laugh, sir, but if this is a sample of your aristocratic—

SPURRELL - If you could only see yourself! But I'd nothing to do with it, 'pon my word I hadn't; only just this minute got away from the hall.... I know! It's that sulky young beggar, Bearpark. I remember he slipped off on some excuse or other just now. He must have come in here and fixed that affair up for me—confound him!

UNDERSHELL - I think I'm the person most entitled to— But no matter; it is merely one insult more among so many. I came here, sir, for a purpose, as you are aware.

SPURRELL - (ruefully). Your dress clothes? All right, you shall have them directly. I wouldn't have put 'em on if I'd known they'd be wanted so soon.

UNDERSHELL - I should have thought your own would have been more comfortable.

SPURRELL - More comfortable! I believe you. Why, I assure you I feel like a Bath bun in a baby's sock! But how was I to know? You shouldn't leave your things about like that!

UNDERSHELL - It is usual, sir, for people to come to a place like this provided with evening clothes of their own.

SPURRELL - I know that as well as you do. Don't you suppose I'm unacquainted with the usages of society! Why, I've stayed in boarding-houses at the seaside many a time where it was de rigger to dress—even for high tea! But coming down, as I did, on business, it never entered my head that I should want my dress suit. So, when I found them all as chummy and friendly as possible, and expecting me to dine as a matter of course,—why, I can tell you I was too jolly glad to get hold of anything in the shape of a swallowtail and white choker to be over particular!

UNDERSHELL - You seem to have been more fortunate in your reception than I. But then I had not the advantage of being here in a business capacity.

SPURRELL - Well, it wasn't that altogether. You see, I'm a kind of a celebrity in my way.

UNDERSHELL - I should hardly have thought that would be a recommendation here.

SPURRELL - I was surprised myself to find what a lot they thought of it; but, bless you, they're all as civil as shopwalkers; and, as for the ladies, why, the old Countess and Lady Maisie and Lady Rhonda couldn't be more complimentary if I'd won the Victoria Cross, instead of getting a first prize for breeding and exhibiting a bull-bitch at Cruft's Dog show!

UNDERSHELL - (bitterly, to himself). And this is our aristocracy! They make a bosom friend of a breeder of dogs; and find a poet only fit to associate with their servants! What a theme for a satirist! (Aloud.) I see nothing to wonder at. You possess precisely the social qualifications most likely to appeal to the leisured class.

SPURRELL - Oh, there's a lot of humbug in it, mind you! Most of 'em know about as much of the points of a bull as the points of a compass, only they let on to know a lot because they think it's smart. And some of 'em are after a pup from old Drummy's next litter. I see through all that, you know!

UNDERSHELL - You are a cynic, I observe, sir. But possibly the nature of the business which brings you here renders them—

SPURRELL - That's the rummest thing about it. I haven't heard a word about that yet. I'm in the veterinary profession, you know. Well, they sent for me to see some blooming horse, and never even ask me to go near it! Seems odd, don't it?

UNDERSHELL - (to himself). I had to go near the blooming horse! Now I begin to understand; the very servants did not expect to find a professional vet in any company but their own! (Aloud.) I—I trust that the horse will not suffer through any delay.

SPURRELL - So do I; but how do I know that some ignorant duffer mayn't be treating him for the wrong thing? It may be all up with the animal before I get a chance of seeing what I can do?

UNDERSHELL - (to himself). If he knew how near I went to getting the poor beast shot! But I needn't mention that now.

SPURRELL - I don't say it isn't gratifying to be treated like a swell, but I've got my professional reputation to consider, you know; and if they're going to take up all my time talking about Andromeda—

UNDERSHELL - (with a start). Andromeda! They have been talking about Andromeda? To you! Then it's you who—

SPURRELL - Haven't I been telling you? I should just jolly well think they have been talking about her! So you didn't know my bull's name was Andromeda before, eh? But you seem to have heard of her, too!

UNDERSHELL - (slowly). I—I have heard of Andromeda—yes.

[He drops into a chair, dazed.

SPURRELL - (complacently). It's curious how that bitch's fame seems to have spread. Why, even the old Bishop— But, I say, you're looking rather queer; anything the matter with you, old fellow?

UNDERSHELL - (faintly). Nothing—nothing. I—I feel a little giddy, that's all. I shall be better presently.

[He conceals his face.

SPURRELL - (in concern). It was having that basket down on your head like that. Too bad! Here, I'll get you some water. (He bustles about.) I don't know if you're aware of it, old chap, but you're in a regular dooce of a mess!

UNDERSHELL - (motioning him away irritably). Do you suppose I don't know that? For Heaven's sake, don't speak to me! let me alone!... I want to think—I want to think. (To himself.) I see it all now! I've made a hideous mistake! I thought these Culverins were deliberately— And all the time— Oh, what an unspeakable idiot I've been!... And I can't even explain!... The only thing to do is to escape before this fellow suspects the truth. It's lucky I ordered that carriage! (Aloud, rising.) I'm all right now; and—and I can't stay here any longer. I am leaving directly—directly!

SPURRELL - You must give me time to get out of this toggery, old chap; you'll have to pick me out of it like a lobster!

UNDERSHELL - (wildly). The clothes? Never mind them now. I can't wait. Keep them!

SPURRELL - Do you really mean it, old fellow? If you could spare 'em a bit longer, I'd be no end obliged. Because, you see, I promised LADY RHONDA to come and finish a talk we were having, and they've taken away my own things to brush, so I haven't a rag to go down in except these; and they'd all think it so beastly rude if I went to bed now!

UNDERSHELL - (impatiently). I tell you you may keep them, if you'll only go away!

SPURRELL - But where am I to send the things to when I've done with 'em?

UNDERSHELL - What do I— Stay, here's my card. Send them to that address. Now go and finish your evening!

SPURRELL - (gratefully). You are a rattling good chap, and no mistake! Though I'm hanged if I can quite make out what you're doing here, you know!

UNDERSHELL - It's not at all necessary that you should make it out. I am leaving immediately, and—and I don't wish Sir Rupert or Lady Culverin to hear of this—you understand?

SPURRELL - Well, it's no business of mine; you've behaved devilish well to me, and I'm not surprised that you'd rather not be seen in the state you're in. I shouldn't like it myself!

UNDERSHELL - State? What state?

SPURRELL - Ah, I wondered whether you knew. You'll see what I mean when you've had a look at yourself in the glass. I dare say it'll come off right enough. I can't stop. Ta, ta, old fellow, and thanks awfully!

[He goes out.

UNDERSHELL - (alone). What does he mean? But I've no time to waste. Where have they put my portmanteau? I can't give up everything. (He hunts round the room, and eventually discovers a door leading into a small dressing-room.) Ah, it's in there. I'll get it out, and put my things in. (As he rushes back, he suddenly comes face to face with his own reflection in a cheval glass.) Wh—who's that? Can this—this piebald horror possibly be—me? How—? Ah, it was ink in that infernal basket—not water! And my hair's full of flour! I can't go into a hotel like this, they'd think I was an escaped lunatic! (He flies to a wash-hand stand, and scrubs and sluices desperately, after which he inspects the result in the mirror.) It's not nearly off yet! Will anything get rid of this streakiness? (He soaps and scrubs once more.) And the flour's caked in my hair now! I must brush it all out before I am fit to be seen. (He gradually, after infinite toil, succeeds in making himself slightly more presentable.) Is the carriage waiting for me all this time? (He pitches things into his portmanteau in a frantic flurry.) What's that? Some one's coming!

[He listens.

TREDWELL - (outside). It's my conviction you've been telling me a pack o' lies, you young rascal. For what hearthly business that feller Undershell could 'ave in the Verney— However, I'll soon see how it is. (He knocks.) Is any one in 'ere?

UNDERSHELL - (to himself, distractedly). He mustn't find me here! Yet, where— Ah, it's the only place!

[He blows out the candles, and darts into the dressing-room as TREDWELL enters.

TREDWELL - The boy's right. He is in here; them candles is smouldering still. (He relights one, and looks under the bed.) You'd better come out o' that, Undershell, and give an account of yourself—do you 'ear me?... He ain't under there! (He tries the dressing-room door; UNDERSHELL holds his breath, and clings desperately to the handle.) Very well, sir, I know you're there, and I've no time to trouble with you at present, so you may as well stay where you are till you're wanted. I've 'eard o' your goings-on from Mr. Adams, and I shall 'ave to fetch Sir Rupert up to 'ave a talk with you by and bye.

[He turns the key upon him, and goes.

UNDERSHELL - (to himself, overwhelmed, as the butler's step is heard retreating.) And I came down here to assert the dignity of Literature!

## PART XVI

## AN INTELLECTUAL PRIVILEGE

In the Chinese Drawing-room.

TIME—About 9.45 P.M.

MRS EARWAKER - Yes, dear Lady Lullington, I've always insisted on each of my girls adopting a distinct line of her own, and the result has been most satisfactory. Louisa, my eldest, is literary; she had a little story accepted not long ago by The Milky Way; then Maria is musical—practices regularly three hours every day on her violin. Fanny has become quite an expert in photography—kodaked her father the other day in the act of trying a difficult stroke at billiards; a back view—but so clever and characteristic!

LADY LULLINGTON - (absently). A back view? How nice!

MRS EARWAKER - He was the only one of the family who didn't recognize it at once. Then my youngest Caroline—well, I must say that for a long time I was quite in despair about Caroline. It really looked as if there was no single thing that she had the slightest bent or inclination for. So at last I thought she had better take up religion, and make that her speciality.

LADY LULLINGTON - (languidly). Religion! How very nice!

MRS EARWAKER - Well, I got her a Christian Year and a covered basket, and quantities of tracts, and so on; but, somehow, she didn't seem to get on with it. So I let her give it up; and now she's gone in for poker-etching instead.

LADY LULLINGTON - (by an act of unconscious cerebration). Poker-etching! How very, very nice!

[Her eyelids close gently.

LADY RHONDA - Oh, but indeed, Lady Culverin, I thought he was perfectly charmin': not a bit booky, you know, but as clever as he can stick; knows more about terriers than any man I ever met!

LADY CULVERIN - So glad you found him agreeable, my dear. I was half afraid he might strike you as— well, just a little bit common in his way of talking.

LADY RHONDA - P'raps—but, after all, one can't expect those sort of people to talk quite like we do ourselves, can one?

LADY CANTIRE - Is that Mr. Spurrell you are finding fault with, Albinia? It is curious that you should be the one person here who— I consider him a very worthy and talented young man, and I shall most certainly ask him to dinner—or lunch, at all events—as soon as we return. I dare say Lady Rhonda will not object to come and meet him.

LADY RHONDA - Rather not. I'll come, like a shot!

LADY CULERIN - (to herself). I suppose it's very silly of me to be so prejudiced. Nobody else seems to mind him!

MISS SPELWANE - (crossing over to them). Oh, Lady Culverin, Lady Lullington has such a delightful idea—she's just been saying how very, very nice it would be if Mr. Spurrell could be persuaded to read some of his poetry aloud to us presently. Do you think it could be managed?

LADY CULERIN - (in distress) Really, my dear Vivien, I—I don't know what to say. I fancy people would so much rather talk—don't you think so, Rohesia?

LADY CANTIRE - Probably they would, Albinia. It is most unlikely that they would care to hear anything more intellectual and instructive than the sound of their own voices.

MISS SPELWANE - I told Lady Lullington that I was afraid you would think it a bore, Lady Cantire.

LADY CANTIRE - You are perfectly mistaken, Miss Spelwane. I flatter myself I am quite as capable of appreciating a literary privilege as anybody here. But I cannot answer for its being so acceptable to the majority.

LADY CULVERIN - No, it wouldn't do at all. And it would be making this young man so much too conspicuous.

LADY CANTIRE - You are talking nonsense, my dear. When you are fortunate enough to secure a celebrity at Wyvern, you can't make him too conspicuous. I never knew that Laura Lullington had any taste for literature before, but there's something to be said for her suggestion—if it can be carried out; it would at least provide a welcome relief from the usual after-dinner dullness of this sort of gathering.

MISS SPELWANE - Then—would you ask him, Lady Cantire?

LADY CANTIRE - I, my dear? You forget that I am not hostess here. My sister-in-law is the proper person to do that.

LADY CULVERIN - Indeed I couldn't. But perhaps, Vivien, if you liked to suggest it to him, he might—

MISS SPELWANE - I'll try, dear Lady Culverin. And if my poor little persuasions have no effect, I shall fall back on Lady Cantire, and then he can't refuse. I must go and tell dear Lady Lullington—she'll be so pleased! (To herself, as she skims away.) I generally do get my own way. But I mean him to do it to please Me!

LADY CANTIRE - (to herself) I must say that girl is very much improved in manner since I last saw anything of her.

MRS CHATTERIS - (a little later, to LADY MAISIE) Have you heard what a treat is in store for us? That delightful Mr. Spurrell is going to give us a reading or a recitation, or something, from his own poems; at least Miss Spelwane is to ask him as soon as the men come in. Only I should have thought that he would be much more likely to consent if you asked him.

LADY MAISIE - Would you? I'm sure I don't know why.

MRS CHATTERIS - (archly). Oh, he took me in to dinner, you know, and it's quite wonderful how people confide in me, but I suppose they feel I can be trusted. He mentioned a little fact, which gave me the impression that a certain fair lady's wishes would be supreme with him.

LADY MAISIE - (to herself). The wretch! He has been boasting of my unfortunate letter! (Aloud.) Mr. Spurrell had no business to give you any impression of the kind. And the mere fact that I—that I happened to admire his verses—

MRS CHATTERIS - Exactly! Poets' heads are so easily turned; and, as I said to Captain Thicknesse—

LADY MAISIE - Captain Thicknesse! You have been talking about it—to him!

MRS CHATTERIS - I'd no idea you would mind anybody knowing, or I would never have dreamed of— I've such a perfect horror of gossip! It took me so much by surprise, that I simply couldn't resist. But I can easily tell Captain Thicknesse It was all a mistake; he knows how fearfully inaccurate I always am.

LADY MAISIE - I would rather you said nothing more about it, please; it is really not worth while contradicting anything so utterly absurd. (To herself.) That Gerald—Captain Thicknesse—of all people, should know of my letter! And goodness only knows what story she may have made out of it!

MRS CHATTERIS - (to herself, as she moves away). I've been letting my tongue run away with me, as usual. She's not the original of "Lady Grisoline," after all. Perhaps he meant Vivien Spelwane—the description was much more like her!

PILLINER - (who has just entered with some of the younger men, to Miss SPELWANE). What are you doing with these chairs? Why are we all to sit in a circle, like Moore and Burgess people? You're not going to set the poor dear Bishop down to play baby-games? How perfectly barbarous of you!

MISS SPELWANE - The chairs are being arranged for something much more intellectual. We are going to get Mr. Spurrell to read a poem to us, if you want to know. I told you I should manage it.

PILLINER - There's only one drawback to that highly desirable arrangement. The songster has unostentatiously retired to roost. So I'm afraid you'll have to do without your poetry this evening—that is, unless you care to avail yourself again of my services?

MISS SPELWANE - (indignantly). It is too mean of you. You must have told him!

[He protests his innocence.

LADY RHONDA - Archie, what's become of Mr. Spurrell? I particularly want to ask him something.

ARCHIE BEARPARK - The poet? He nipped upstairs—as I told you all along he meant to—to scribble some of his democratic drivel, and (with a suppressed grin) I don't think you'll see him again this evening.

CAPTAIN THICKNESSE - (to himself, as he enters). She's keepin' a chair next hers in the corner there for somebody. Can it be for that poet chap?... (He meets LADY MAISIE'S eye suddenly.) Great Scott! If she means it for me!... I've half a mind not to— No, I shall be a fool if I lose such a chance! (He crosses, and drops into the vacant chair next hers.) I may sit here, mayn't I?

LADY MAISIE - (simply). I meant you to. We used to be such good friends; it's a pity to have misunderstandings. And—and I want to ask you what that silly little Mrs. Chatteris has been telling you at dinner about me.

CAPTAIN THICKNESSE - Well, she was sayin'—and I must say I don't understand it, after your tellin' me you knew nothing about this Mr. Spurrell till this afternoon—

LADY MAISIE - But I don't. And I—I did offer to explain, but you said you weren't curious!

CAPTAIN THICKNESSE - Didn't want you to tell me anything that perhaps you'd rather not, don't you know. Still, I should like to know how this poet chap came to write a poem all about you, and call it "Lady Grisoline," if he never—

LADY MAISIE - But it's too ridiculous! How could he? When he never saw me, so far as I know, in all his life before!

CAPTAIN THICKNESSE - He told Mrs. Chatteris you were the original of his "Lady Grisoline" anyway, and really—

LADY MAISIE - He dared to tell her that? How disgracefully impertinent of him. (To herself.) So long as he hasn't talked about my letter, he may say what he pleases!

CAPTAIN THICKNESSE - But what was it you were goin' to explain to me? You said there was somethin'—

LADY MAISIE - (to herself). It's no use; I'd sooner die than tell him about that letter now! (Aloud.) I—I only wished you to understand that, whatever I think about poetry—I detest poets!

LADY CANTIRE - Yes, as you say, Bishop, a truly Augustan mode of recreation. Still, Mr. Spurrell doesn't seem to have come in yet, so I shall have time to hear anything you have to say in defence of your opposition to Parish Councils.

[THE BISHOP resigns himself to the inevitable.

ARCHIE BEARPARK - (in PILLINER'S ear). Ink and flour—couldn't possibly miss him; the bard's got a matted head this time, and no mistake.

PILLINER - Beastly bad form, I call it—with a fellow you don't know. You'll get yourself into trouble some day. And you couldn't even bring your own ridiculous booby-trap off, for here the beggar comes, as if nothing had happened.

ARCHIE BEARPARK - (disconcerted). Confound him! The best booby trap I ever made!

THE BISHOP - My dear Lady Cantire, here is our youthful poet, at the eleventh hour. (To himself.) "Sic me servavit Apollo!"

[Miss SPELWANE advances to meet SPURRELL, who stands surveying the array of chairs in blank bewilderment.

## PART XVII

A BOMB SHELL

In a Gallery near the Verney Chamber.

TIME—Same as that of the preceding Part.

SPURRELL - (to himself). I must say it's rather rough luck on that poor devil. I get his dress suit, and all he comes in for is my booby-trap! (PHILLIPSON, wearing a holland blouse over her evening toilette, approaches from the other end of the passage; he does not recognise her until the moment of collision.) Emma!! It's never you! How do you come to be here?

PHILLIPSON - (to herself). Then it was my Jem after all! (Aloud, distantly.) I'm here in attendance on Lady Maisie Mull, being her maid. If I was at all curious—which I'm not—I might ask you what you're doing in such a house as this; and in evening dress, if you please!

SPURRELL - I'm in evening dress, Emma, such as it is (not that I've any right to find fault with it); but I'm in evening dress (with dignity) because I've been included in the dinner party here.

PHILLIPSON - You must have been getting on since I knew you. Then you were studying to be a horse-doctor.

SPURRELL - I have got on. I am now a qualified M.R.C.V.S.

PHILLIPSON - And does that qualify you to dine with bishops and countesses and baronets and the gentry, like one of themselves?

SPURRELL - I don't say it does, in itself. It was my Andromeda that did the trick, Emma.

PHILLIPSON - Andromeda? They were talking of that downstairs. What made you take to scribbling, James?

SPURRELL - Scribbling? how do you mean? My handwriting's easy enough to read, as you ought to know very well.

PHILLIPSON - You can't expect me to remember what your writing's like; it's so long since I've seen it!

SPURRELL - Come, I like that! When I wrote twice to say I was sorry we'd fallen out; and never got a word back!

PHILLIPSON - If you'd written to the addresses I gave you abroad—

SPURRELL - Then you did write; but none of the letters reached me. I never even knew you'd gone abroad. I wrote to the old place. And so did you, I suppose, not knowing I'd moved my lodgings too, so naturally— But what does it all matter, so long as we've met and it's all right between us? Oh, my dear girl, if you only knew how I worried myself, thinking you were— Well, all that's over now, isn't it?

[He attempts to embrace her.

PHILLIPSON - (repulsing him). Not quite so fast, James. Before I say whether we're to be as we were or not, I want to know a little more about you. You wouldn't be here like this if you hadn't done something to distinguish yourself.

SPURRELL - Well, I don't say I mayn't have got a certain amount of what they call "kudosh," owing to Andromeda. But what difference does that make?

PHILLIPSON - Tell me, James, is it you that's been writing a pink book all over silver cutlets?

SPURRELL - Me? Write a book—about cutlets—or anything else! Emma, you don't suppose I've quite come down to that! Andromeda's the name of my bull-dog. I took first prize with her; there were portraits of both of us in one of the papers. And the people here were very much taken with the dog, and—and so they asked me to dine with them. That's how it was.

PHILLIPSON - I should have thought, if they asked one of you to dine, it ought to have been the bull-dog.

SPURRELL - Now what's the good of saying extravagant things of that sort? Not that old Drummy couldn't be trusted to behave anywhere!

PHILLIPSON - Better than her master, I dare say. I heard of your goings on with some LADY RHONDA or other!

SPURRELL - Oh, the girl I sat next to at dinner? Nice chatty sort of girl; seems fond of quadrupeds—

PHILLIPSON - Especially two-legged ones! You see, I've been told all about it!

SPURRELL - I assure you, I didn't go a step beyond the most ordinary civility. You're not going to be jealous because I promised I'd give her a liniment for one of her dogs, are you?

PHILLIPSON - Liniment! You always were a flirt, James! But I'm not jealous. I've met a very nice-spoken young man while I've been here; he sat next to me at supper, and paid me the most beautiful compliments, and was most polite and attentive—though he hasn't got as far as liniment, at present.

SPURRELL - But, Emma, you're not going to take up with some other fellow just when we've come together again?

PHILLIPSON - If you call it "coming together," when I'm down in the housekeeper's room, and you're up above, carrying on with ladies of title!

SPURRELL - Do you want to drive me frantic? As if I could help being where I am! How could I know you were here?

PHILLIPSON - At all events, you know now, James. And it's for you to choose between your smart lady friends and me. If you're fit company for them, you're too grand for one of their maids.

SPURRELL - My dear girl, don't be unreasonable! I'm expected back in the drawing-room, and I can't throw 'em over now all of a sudden without giving offence. There's the interests of the firm to consider, and it's not for me to take a lower place than I'm given. But it's only for a night or two, and you don't really suppose I wouldn't rather be where you are if I was free to choose—but I'm not, Emma, that's the worst of it!

PHILLIPSON - Well, go back to the drawing-room, then; don't keep Lady Rhonda waiting for her liniment on my account. I ought to be in my ladies' rooms by this time. Only don't be surprised if, whenever you are free to choose, you find you've come back just too late—that's all!

[She turns to leave him.

SPURRELL - (detaining her). Emma, I won't let you go like this! Not before you've told me where I can meet you again here.

PHILLIPSON - There's no place that I know of—except the housekeeper's room; and of course you couldn't descend so low as that.... James, there's somebody coming! Let go my hand—do you want to lose me my character!

[Steps and voices are heard at the other end of the passage; she frees herself, and escapes.

SPURRELL - (attempting to follow). But, Emma, stop one— She's gone!... Confound it, there's the butler and a page-boy coming! It's no use staying up here any longer. (To himself, as he goes downstairs.) It's downright torture—that's what it is! To be tied by the leg in the drawing-room, doing the civil to a lot of girls I don't care a blow about; and to know that all the time some blarneying beggar downstairs is doing his best to rob me of my Emma! Flesh and blood can't stand it; and yet I'm blest if I see any way out of it without offending 'em all round.

[He enters the Chinese Drawing-room.

In the Chinese Drawing-room.

MISS SPELWANE - At last, Mr. Spurrell! We began to think you meant to keep away altogether. Has anybody told you why you've been waited for so impatiently?

SPURRELL - (looking round the circle of chairs apprehensively). No. Is it family prayers, or what? Er—are they over?

MISS SPELWANE - No, no; nothing of that sort. Can't you guess? Mr. Spurrell, I'm going to be very bold, and ask a great, great favour of you. I don't know why they chose me to represent them; I told Lady Lullington I was afraid my entreaties would have no weight; but if you only would—

SPURRELL - (to himself). They're at it again! How many more of 'em want a pup! (Aloud.) Sorry to be disobliging, but—

MISS SPELWANE - (joining her hands in supplication). Not if I implore you? Oh, Mr. Spurrell, I've quite set my heart on hearing you read aloud to us. Are you really cruel enough to refuse?

SPURRELL - Read aloud! Is that what you want me to do? But I'm no particular hand at it. I don't know that I've ever read aloud—except a bit out of the paper now and then—since I was a boy at school!

LADY CANTIRE - What's that I hear? Mr. Spurrell professing incapacity to read aloud? Sheer affectation! Come, Mr. Spurrell, I am much mistaken if you are wanting in the power to thrill all hearts here. Think of us as instruments ready to respond to your touch. Play upon us as you will; but don't be so ungracious as to raise any further obstacles.

SPURRELL - (resignedly). Oh, very well, if I'm required to read, I'm agreeable.

[Murmurs of satisfaction.

LADY CANTIRE - Hush, please, everybody! Mr. Spurrell is going to read. My dear Bishop, if you wouldn't mind just— Lord Lullington, can you hear where you are? Where are you going to sit, Mr. Spurrell? In the centre will be best. Will somebody move that lamp a little, so as to give him more light?

SPURRELL - (to himself, as he sits down). I wonder what we're supposed to be playing at! (Aloud.) Well, what am I to read, eh?

MISS SPELWANE - (placing an open copy of "Andromeda" in his hands with a charming air of deferential dictation). You might begin with this—such a dear little piece! I'm dying to hear you read it!

SPURRELL - (as he takes the book). I'll do the best I can! (He looks at the page in dismay.) Why, look here, it's poetry! I didn't bargain for that. Poetry's altogether out of my line!

[Miss SPELWANE opens her eyes to their fullest extent, and retires a few paces from him; he begins to read in a perfunctory monotone, with deepening bewilderment and disgust—

"THE SICK KNIGHT.

Reach me the helmet from yonder rack,
Mistress o' mine! with its plume of white:
Now help me upon my destrier's back,
Mistress o' mine! though he swerve in fright.
And guide my foot to the stirrup-ledge,
Mistress o' mine! it eludes me still.
Then fill me a cup as a farewell pledge,
Mistress o' mine! for the night air's chill!
Haste! with the buckler and pennon'd lance,
Mistress o' mine! or ever I feel
My war-horse plunge in impatient prance,
Mistress o' mine! at the prick of heel.
Pay scant heed to my pallid hue,
Mistress o' mine! for the wan moon's sheen

Doth blazon the gules o' my cheek with blue,
Mistress o' mine! or glamour it green.
One last long kiss, ere I seek the fray ...
Mistress o' mine! though I quit my sell,
I would meet the foe i' the mad mêlée.
Mistress o' mine! an' I were but well!"

(After the murmur of conventional appreciation has died away.) Well, of course, I don't set up for a judge of such things myself, but I must say, if I was asked my opinion—of all the downright tommy-rot I ever— (The company look at one another with raised eyebrows and dropped underlips; he turns over the leaves backwards until he arrives at the title-page.) I say, though, I do call this rather rum! Who the dickens is Clarion Blair? Because I never heard of him—and yet it seems he's been writing poetry on my bull-dog!

MISS SPELWANE - (faintly). Writing poetry—about your bull-dog!

SPURRELL - Yes, the one you've all been praising up so. If it isn't meant for her, it's what you might call a most surprising coincidence, for here's the old dog's name as plain as it can be—Andromeda!

[Tableau.


PART XVIII

THE LAST STRAW

After SPURRELL'S ingenuous comments upon the volume in his hand, a painful silence ensues, which no one has sufficient presence of mind to break for several seconds.

MISS SPELWANE - (to herself). Not Clarion Blair! Not even a poet! I—I could slap him!

PILLINER - (to himself). Poor dear Vivien! But if people will insist on patting a strange poet, they mustn't be surprised if they get a nasty bite!

LADY MAISIE - (to herself). He didn't write Andromeda! Then he hasn't got my letter after all! And I've been such a brute to the poor dear man! How lucky I said nothing about it to Gerald!

CAPTAIN THICKNESSE - (to himself). So he ain't the bard!... Now I see why Maisie's been behavin' so oddly all the evenin'; she spotted him, and didn't like to speak out. Tried to give me a hint, though. Well, I shall stay out my leave now!

LADY RHONDA - (to herself). I thought all along he seemed too good a sort for a poet!

ARCHIE BEARPARK - (to himself). It's all very well; but how about that skit he went up to write on us? He must be a poet of sorts.

MRS BROOKE-CHATTERIS - (to herself). This is fearfully puzzling. What made him say that about "Lady Grisoline"?

THE BISHOP - (to himself). A crushing blow for the Countess; but not unsalutary. I am distinctly conscious of feeling more kindly disposed to that young man. Now why?

[He ponders.

LADY LULLINGTON - (to herself). I thought this young man was going to read us some more of his poetry; it's too tiresome of him to stop to tell us about his bull-dog. As if anybody cared what he called it!

LORD LULLINGTON - (to himself). Uncommonly awkward, this! If I could catch Laura's eye—but I suppose it would hardly be decent to go just yet.

LADY CULERIN - (to herself). Can Rohesia have known this? What possible object could she have had in— And oh, dear, how disgusted Rupert will be!

SIR RUPERT CULVERIN - (to himself). Seems a decent young chap enough! Too bad of Rohesia to let him in for this. I don't care a straw what he is—he's none the worse for not being a poet.

LADY CANTIRE - (to herself). What is he maundering about? It's utterly inconceivable that I should have made any mistake. It's only too clear what the cause is—Claret!

SPURRELL - (aloud, good-humouredly). Too bad of you to try and spoof me like this before everybody, Miss Spelwane! I don't know whose idea it was to play me such a trick, but—

MISS SPELWANE - (indistinctly). Please understand that nobody here had the least intention of playing a trick upon you!

SPURRELL - Well, if you say so, of course— But it looked rather like it, asking me to read when I've about as much poetry in me as—as a pot hat! Still, if I'm wanted to read aloud, I shall be happy to—

LADY CULERIN - (hastily). Indeed, indeed, Mr. Spurrell, we couldn't think of troubling you any more under the circumstances! (In desperation.) Vivien, my dear, won't you sing something?

[The company echo the request with unusual eagerness.

SPURRELL - (to himself, during MISS SPELWANE'S song). Wonder what's put them off being read to all of a sudden? My elocution mayn't be first-class, exactly, but still— (As his eye happens to rest on the binding of the volume on his knee.) Hullo! This cover's pink, with silver things, not unlike cutlets, on it! Didn't Emma ask me—? By George, if it's that! I may get down to the housekeeper's room, after all! As soon as ever this squalling stops I'll find out; I can't go on like this! (MISS SPELWANE leaves the piano; everybody plunges feverishly into conversation on the first subject—other than poetry or dogs—that presents itself, until LORD and LADY LULLINGTON set a welcome example of departure.) Better wait till these county nobs have cleared, I suppose—there goes the last of 'em—now for it!... (He pulls himself together, and approaches his host and hostess.) Hem, Sir Rupert, and your ladyship, it's occurred to me that it's just barely possible you may have got it in your heads that I was something in the poetical way.

SIR RUPERT CULVERIN - (to himself). Not this poor young chap's fault; must let him down as easily as possible! (Aloud.) Not at all—not at all! Ha—assure you we quite understand; no necessity to say another word about it.

SPURRELL - (to himself). Just my luck! They quite understand! No housekeeper's room for me this journey! (Aloud.) Of course I knew the Countess, there, and Lady Maisie, were fully aware all along— (To Lady MAISIE, as stifled exclamations reach his ear.) You were, weren't you?

LADY MAISIE - (hastily). Yes, yes, Mr. SPURRELL - Of course! It's all perfectly right!

SPURRELL - (to the others). You see, I should never have thought of coming in as a visitor if it hadn't been for the Countess; she would have it that it was all right, and that I needn't be afraid I shouldn't be welcome.

LADY CULVERIN - To be sure—any friend of my sister-in-law's—

LADY CANTIRE - Albinia, I have refrained from speech as long as possible; but this is really too much! You don't suppose I should have introduced Mr. Spurrell here unless I had had the strongest reasons for knowing, however he may be pleased to mystify us now, that he, and nobody else, is the author of Andromeda! And I, for one, absolutely decline to believe in this preposterous story of his about a bull-dog.

SPURRELL - But your ladyship must have known! Why, you as good as asked me on the way here to put you down for a bull-pup!

LADY CANTIRE - Never, never! A bull-pup is the last creature I should ever dream of coveting. You were obliging enough to ask me to accept a presentation copy of your verses.

SPURRELL - Was I? I don't exactly see how I could have been, considering I never made a rhyme in my life!

SIR RUPERT CULVERIN - There, there, Rohesia, it was your mistake; but as we are indebted to it for the pleasure of making Mr. Spurrell's acquaintance—

LADY CANTIRE - I am not in the habit of making mistakes, Rupert. I don't know what you and Albinia and Maisie may know that I am in ignorance of, but, since you seem to have been aware from the first that Mr. Spurrell was not the poet you had invited here to meet me, will you kindly explain what has become of the real author?

SIR RUPERT CULVERIN - My dear Rohesia, I don't know and I don't care!

LADY CANTIRE - There you are wrong, Rupert, because it's obvious that if he is not Mr. Spurrell, the real poet's absence has to be accounted for in some way.

SPURRELL - By Jove, I believe I can put you on the track. I shouldn't wonder if he's the party these dress clothes of mine belong to! I dare say you may have noticed they don't look as if they were made for me?

LADY CANTIRE - (closing her eyes). Pray let us avoid any sartorial questions! We are waiting to hear about this person.

SPURRELL - Well, I found I'd got on his things by mistake, and I went up as soon as I could after dessert to my room to take 'em off, and there he was, with a waste-paper basket on his head—

LADY CANTIRE - A waste-paper basket on his head! And pray what should he have that for?

SPURRELL - I'm no wiser than your ladyship there. All I know is he said he wouldn't take it off till he saw me. And I never saw any one in such a mess with ink and flour as he was!

LADY CANTIRE - Ink and flour, indeed! This rigmarole gets more ridiculous every moment! You can't seriously expect any one here to believe it!

[ARCHIE discreetly retires to the smoking-room.

SPURRELL - Well, I rather think somebody must have fixed up a booby-trap for me, you know, and he happened to go in first and get the benefit of it. And he was riled, very naturally, thinking I'd done it, but after we'd had a little talk together, he calmed down and said I might keep his clothes, which I thought uncommonly good-natured of him, you know. By the way, he gave me his card. Here it is, if your ladyship would like to see it.

[He hands it to LADY CULVERIN.

LADY CULVERIN - "Mr. Undershell!"... Rohesia, that is Clarion Blair! I knew it was something ending in "ell." (To SPURRELL.) And you say Mr. Undershell is here—in this house?

SPURRELL - Not now. He's gone by this time.

THE OTHERS - (in dismay). Gone!

SPURRELL - He said he was leaving at once. If he'd only told me how it was, I'd have—

LADY CANTIRE - I don't believe a single word of all this! If Mr. Spurrell is not Clarion Blair, let him explain how he came to be coming down to Wyvern this afternoon!

SPURRELL - If your ladyship doesn't really know, you had better ask Sir Rupert; he'll tell you it's all right.

LADY CANTIRE - Then perhaps you will be good enough to enlighten us, Rupert?

SIR RUPERT CULVERIN - (driven into a corner). Why, 'pon my word, I'm bound to say that I'm just as much in the dark as anybody else, if it comes to that!

SPURRELL - (eagerly). But you wired me to come, sir! About a horse of yours! I've been wondering all the evening when you'd tell me I could go round and have a look at him. I'm here instead of Mr. Spavin— now do you understand, Sir Rupert? I'm the vet.

[Suppressed sensation.

SIR RUPERT CULVERIN - (to himself). This is devilish awkward! Don't quite know what to do. (Aloud.) To—to be sure you are! Of course! That's it, Rohesia! Mr. Spurrell came down to see a horse, and we shall be very glad to have the benefit of his opinion by and bye.

[He claps him amicably on the shoulder.

LADY CANTIRE - (in a sepulchral tone). Albinia, I think I will go to bed.

[She withdraws.

SIR RUPERT CULVERIN - (to himself). There'll be no harm in letting him stay, now he is here. If Rohesia objects, she's got nobody but herself to blame for it!

SPURRELL - (to himself). They won't want to keep me upstairs much longer after this! (TREDWELL enters, and seems to have something of importance to communicate to SIR RUPERT in private.) I wonder what the dooce is up now!

[Partial reaction in company.


PART XIX

UNEARNED INCREMENT

SIR RUPERT - (to TREDWELL). Well, what is it?

TREDWELL - (in an undertone). With reference to the party, Sir Rupert, as represents himself to have come down to see the 'orse, I—

SIR RUPERT CULVERIN - (aloud). You mean Mr. Spurrell? It's all right. Mr. Spurrell will see the horse to-morrow. (TREDWELL disguises his utter bewilderment.) By the way, we expected a Mr. — What did you say the name was, my dear?... Undershell? To be sure, a Mr. Undershell, to have been here in time for dinner. Do you know why he has been unable to come before this?

TREDWELL - (to himself). Do I know? Oh, Lor! (Aloud.) I—I believe he have arrived, Sir Rupert.

SIR RUPERT CULVERIN - So I understand from Mr. Spurrell. Is he here still?

TREDWELL - He is, Sir-I-I considered it my dooty not to allow him to leave the house, not feeling—

SIR RUPERT CULVERIN - Quite right, Tredwell. I should have been most seriously annoyed if I had found that a guest we were all anxiously expecting had left the Court, owing to some fancied—Where is he now?

TREDWELL - (faintly). In—in the Verney Chamber. Leastways—

SIR RUPERT CULVERIN - Ah. (He glances at SPURRELL.) Then where—? But that can be arranged. Go up and explain to Mr. Undershell that we have only this moment heard of his arrival; say we understand that he has been obliged to come by a later train, and that we shall be delighted to see him, just as he is.

SPURRELL - (to himself) He was worth looking at just as he was, when I saw him!

PILLINER - (to himself) By a later train? Then, how the deuce did his clothes—? Oh, well, however it was, it don't concern me.

TREDWELL - Very good, Sir. (To himself, as he departs.) If I'm not precious careful over this job, it may cost me my situation!

SPURRELL - Sir Rupert, I've been thinking that, after what's occurred, it would probably be more satisfactory to all parties if I shifted my quarters, and—took my meals in the housekeeper's room.

[LADY MAISIE and LADY RHONDA utter inarticulate protests.

SIR RUPERT CULVERIN - My dear sir, not on any account—couldn't hear of it! My wife, I'm sure, will say the same.

LADY CULERIN - (with an effort). I hope Mr. Spurrell will continue to be our guest precisely as before— that is, if he will forgive us for putting him into another room.

SPURRELL - (to himself). It's no use; I can't get rid of 'em; they stick to me like a lot of blooming burrs! (Aloud, in despair.) Your ladyship is very good, but— Well, the fact is, I've only just found out that a young lady I've long been deeply attached to is in this very house. She's a Miss Emma Phillipson—maid, so I understand, to Lady Maisie—and, without for one moment wishing to draw any comparisons, or to seem ungrateful for all the friendliness I've received, I really and truly would feel myself more comfortable in a circle where I could enjoy rather more of my Emma's society than I can here!

SIR RUPERT CULVERIN - (immensely relieved). Perfectly natural! and—hum—sorry as we are to lose you, Mr. Spurrell, we—ah—mustn't be inconsiderate enough to keep you here a moment longer. I've no doubt you will find the young lady in the housekeeper's room—any one will tell you where it is.... Good night to you, then; and, remember, we shall expect to see you in the field on Tuesday.

LADY MAISIE - Good night, Mr. Spurrell, and—and I'm so very glad—about Emma, you know. I hope you will both be very happy.

[She shakes hands warmly.

LADY RHONDA - So do I. And mind you don't forget about that liniment, you know.

CAPTAIN THICKNESSE - (to himself). Maisie don't care a hang! And I was ass enough to fancy— But there, that's all over now!

In the Verney Chamber.

UNDERSHELL - (in the dressing-room, to himself). I wonder how long I've been locked up here—it seems hours! I almost hope they've forgotten me altogether.... Some one has come in.... If it should be Sir Rupert!! Great heavens, what a situation to be found in by one's host!... Perhaps it's only that fellow Spurrell; if so, there's a chance. (The door is unlocked by TREDWELL, who has lighted the candles on the dressing table.) It's the butler again. Well, I shall soon know the worst! (He steps out, blinking, with as much dignity as possible.) Perhaps you will kindly inform me why I have been subjected to this indignity?

TREDWELL - (in perturbation). I think, Mr. Undershell, sir, in common fairness, you'll admit as you've mainly yourself to thank for any mistakes that have occurred; for which I 'asten to express my pussonal regret.

UNDERSHELL - So long as you realise that you have made a mistake, I am willing to overlook it, on condition that you help me to get away from this place without your master and mistress's knowledge.

TREDWELL - It's too late, sir. They know you're 'ere!

UNDERSHELL - They know! Then there's no time to be lost. I must leave this moment!

TREDWELL - No, sir, excuse me; but you can't hardly do that now. I was to say that Sir Rupert and the ladies would be glad to see you in the droring-room himmediate.

UNDERSHELL - Man alive! do you imagine anything would induce me to meet them now, after the humiliations I have been compelled to suffer under this roof?

TREDWELL - If you would prefer anything that has taken place in the room, sir, or in the stables to be 'ushed up—

UNDERSHELL - Prefer it! If it were only possible! But they know—they know! What's the use of talking like that?

TREDWELL - (to himself). I know where I am now! (Aloud.) They know nothink up to the present, Mr. Undershell, nor yet I see no occasion why they should—leastwise from any of Us.

UNDERSHELL - But they know I'm here; how am I to account for all the time—?

TREDWELL - Excuse me, sir. I thought of that, and it occurred to me as it might be more agreeable to your feelings, sir, if I conveyed an impression that you had only just arrived—'aving missed your train, sir.

UNDERSHELL - (overjoyed). How am I to thank you? that was really most discreet of you—most considerate!

TREDWELL - I am truly rejoiced to hear you say so, sir. And I'll take care nothing leaks out. And if you'll be kind enough to follow me to the droring-room, the ladies are waiting to see you.

UNDERSHELL - (to himself). I may actually meet Lady Maisie Mull after all! (Aloud, recollecting his condition.) But I can't go down like this. I'm in such a horrible mess!

TREDWELL - I reelly don't perceive it, sir; except a little white on your coat-collar behind. Allow me—there it's off now. (He gives him a hand-glass) If you'd like to see for yourself.

UNDERSHELL - (to himself as he looks). A slight pallor, that's all. I am more presentable than I could have hoped. (Aloud.) Have the kindness to take me to Lady Culverin at once.

In the Chinese Drawing-room. A few minutes later.

SIR RUPERT CULVERIN - (to UNDERSHELL, after the introductions have been gone through). And so you missed the 4.55 and had to come on by the 7.30 which stops everywhere, eh?

UNDERSHELL - It—it certainly does stop at most stations.

SIR RUPERT CULVERIN - And how did you get on to Wyvern—been here long?

UNDERSHELL - N—not particularly long.

SIR RUPERT CULVERIN - Fact is, you see, we made a mistake. Very ridiculous, but we've been taking that young fellow, Mr. Spurrell, for you all this time; so we never thought of inquiring whether you'd come or not. It was only just now he told us how he'd met you in the Verney Chamber, and the very handsome way, if you will allow me to say so, in which you had tried to efface yourself.

UNDERSHELL - (to himself). I didn't expect him to take that view of it! (Aloud.) I—I felt I had no alternative.

[LADY MAISIE regards him with admiration.

SIR RUPERT CULVERIN - You did an uncommon fine thing, sir, and I'm afraid you received treatment on your arrival which you had every right to resent.

UNDERSHELL - (to himself). I hoped he didn't know about the housekeeper's room! (Aloud.) Please say no more about it, Sir. I know now that you were entirely innocent of any—

SIR RUPERT CULVERIN - (horrified). Good Gad! you didn't suppose I had any hand in fixing up that booby-trap, or whatever it was, did you? Young fellows will get bear-fighting and playing idiotic tricks on one another, and you seem to have been the victim—that's how it was. Have you had anything to eat since you came? If not—

UNDERSHELL - (hastily). Thank you, I—I have dined. (To himself.) So he doesn't know where, after all! I will spare him that.

SIR RUPERT CULVERIN - Got some food at Shuntingbridge, eh? Afraid they gave you a wretched dinner?

UNDERSHELL - Quite the reverse, I assure you. (To himself.) Considering that it came from his own table!

PILLINER - (to himself). I still don't understand how his clothes— (Aloud.) Did you send your portmanteau on ahead, then, or what?

UNDERSHELL - (blankly). Send my port—? I don't understand.

PILLINER - Oh, I only asked, because the other man said he was wearing your things.

SIR RUPERT CULVERIN - (as UNDERSHELL remains speechless). I see how it was—perfectly simple—rush for the train—porter put your luggage in—you got left behind, wasn't that it?

UNDERSHELL - I—I certainly did get separated from my portmanteau, somehow, and I suppose it must have arrived before me. (To himself.) Considering the pace of the fly-horse, I think I am justified in assuming that!

PILLINER - (to himself). Ass I was not to hold my tongue!

LADY MAISIE - (in an undertone, to CAPTAIN THICKNESSE). Gerald, you remember what I said some time ago—about poetry and poets?

CAPTAIN THICKNESSE - Perfectly. And I thought you were quite right.

LADY MAISIE - I was quite wrong. I didn't know what I was talking about. I do now. Good night. (She crosses to UNDERSHELL.) Good night, Mr. Blair, I'm so very glad we have met—at last!

[She goes.

UNDERSHELL - (to himself, rapturously). She's not freckled; she's not even sandy. She's lovely! And, by some unhoped-for good fortune, all this has only raised me in her eyes. I am more than compensated!

CAPTAIN THICKNESSE - (to himself). I may just as well get back to Aldershot to-morrow—now. I'll go and prepare Lady C.'s mind, in case. It's hard luck; just when everything seemed goin' right! I'd give somethin' to have the other bard back, I know. It's no earthly use my tryin' to stand against this one!


PART XX

DIFFERENT PERSONS HAVE DIFFERENT OPINIONS

LADY MAISIE'S Room at Wyvern.

TIME—Saturday night, about 11.30.

LADY MAISIE - (to PHILLIPSON, who is brushing her hair). You are sure mamma isn't expecting me? (Irresolutely.) Perhaps I had better just run in and say good night.

PHILLIPSON - I wouldn't recommend it, really, my lady; her ladyship seems a little upset in her nerves this evening.

LADY MAISIE - (to herself). Il-y-a de quoi! (Aloud, relieved.) It might only disturb her, certainly.... I hope they are making you comfortable here, Phillipson?

PHILLIPSON - Very much so indeed, thank you, my lady. The tone of the room downstairs is most superior.

LADY MAISIE - That's satisfactory. And I hear you have met an old admirer of yours here—Mr. Spurrell, I mean.

PHILLIPSON - We did happen to encounter each other in one of the galleries, my lady, just for a minute; though I shouldn't have expected him to allude to it!

LADY MAISIE - Indeed! And why not?

PHILLIPSON - Mr. James Spurrell appears to have elevated himself to a very different sphere from what he occupied when I used to know him, my lady; though how and why he comes to be where he is, I don't rightly understand myself at present.

LADY MAISIE - (to herself). And no wonder! I feel horribly guilty! (Aloud.) You mustn't blame poor Mr. Spurrell, Phillipson; he couldn't help it!

PHILLIPSON - (with studied indifference). I'm not blaming him, my lady. If he prefers the society of his superiors to mine, he's very welcome to do so; there's others only too willing to take his place!

LADY MAISIE - Surely none who would be as fond of you or make so good a husband, Phillipson!

PHILLIPSON - That's as maybe, my lady. There was one young man that travelled down in the same compartment, and sat next me at supper in the room. I could see he took a great fancy to me from the first, and his attentions were really quite pointed. I am sure I couldn't bring myself to repeat his remarks, they were so flattering!

LADY MAISIE - Don't you think you will be rather a foolish girl if you allow a few idle compliments from a stranger to outweigh such an attachment as Mr. Spurrell seems to have for you?

PHILLIPSON - If he's found new friends, my lady, I consider myself free to act similarly.

LADY MAISIE - Then you don't know? He told us quite frankly this evening that he had only just discovered you were here, and would much prefer to be where you were. He went down to the housekeeper's room on purpose.

PHILLIPSON - (moved). It's the first I've heard of it, my lady. It must have been after I came up. If I'd only known he'd behave like that!

LADY MAISIE - (instructively). You see how loyal he is to you. And now, I suppose, he will find he has been supplanted by this new acquaintance—some smooth-tongued, good-for-nothing valet, I dare say?

PHILLIPSON - (injured). Oh, my lady, indeed he wasn't a man! But there was nothing serious between us—at least, on my side—though he certainly did go on in a very sentimental way himself. However, he's left the Court by now, that's one comfort! (To herself.) I wish now I'd said nothing about him to Jem. If he was to get asking questions downstairs— He always was given to jealousy—reason or none!

[A tap is heard at the door.

LADY RHONDA - (outside). Maisie, may I come in? if you've done your hair, and sent away your maid. (She enters.) Ah, I see you haven't.

LADY MAISIE - Don't run away, Rhoda; my maid has just done. You can go now, Phillipson.

LADY RHONDA - (to herself, as she sits down). Phillipson! So that's the young woman that funny vet man prefers to us! H'm, can't say I feel flattered!

PHILLIPSON - (to herself, as she leaves the room). This must be the Lady Rhonda, who was making up to my Jem! He wouldn't have anything to say to her, though; and, now I see her, I am not surprised at it!

[She goes. A pause.

LADY RHONDA - (crossing her feet on the fender). Well, we can't complain of havin' had a dull evenin', can we?

LADY MAISIE - (taking a hand-screen from the mantelshelf). Not altogether. Has—anything fresh happened since I left?

LADY RHONDA - Nothing particular. Archie apologised to this new man in the billiard-room. For the booby trap. We all told him he'd got to. And Mr. Carrion Bear, or Blundershell, or whatever he calls himself—you know—was so awf'lly gracious and condescendin' that I really thought poor dear old Archie would have wound up his apology by punchin' his head for him. Strikes me, Maisie, that mop-headed minstrel boy is a decided change for the worse. Doesn't it you?

LADY MAISIE - (toying with the screen). How do you mean, Rhoda?

LADY RHONDA - I meantersay I call Mr. Spurrell— Well, he's real, anyway—he's a man, don't you know. As for the other, so feeble of him missin' his train like he did, and turnin' up too late for everything! Now, wasn't it?

LADY MAISIE - Poets are dreamy and unpractical and unpunctual—it's their nature.

LADY RHONDA - Then they should stay at home. Just see what a hopeless muddle he's got us all into! I declare I feel as if anybody might turn into somebody else on the smallest provocation after this. I know poor Vivien Spelwane will be worryin' her pillows like rats most of the night, and I rather fancy it will be a close time for poets with your dear mother, Maisie, for some time to come. All this silly little man's fault!

LADY MAISIE - No, Rhoda. Not his—ours. Mine and mamma's. We ought to have felt from the first that there must be some mistake, that poor Mr. Spurrell couldn't possibly be a poet! I don't know, though—people generally are unlike what you'd expect from their books. I believe they do it on purpose! Not that that applies to Mr. Blair; he is one's idea of what a poet should be. If he hadn't arrived when he did, I don't think I could ever have borne to read another line of poetry as long as I lived!

LADY RHONDA - I say! Do you call him as good-lookin' as all that?

LADY MAISIE - I was not thinking about his looks, Rhoda—it's his conduct that's so splendid.

LADY RHONDA - His conduct? Don't see anything splendid in missin' a train. I could do it myself if I tried.

LADY MAISIE - Well, I wish I could think there were many men capable of acting so nobly and generously as he did.

LADY RHONDA - As how?

LADY MAISIE - You really don't see! Well, then, you shall. He arrives late, and finds that somebody else is here already in his character. He makes no fuss; manages to get a private interview with the person who is passing as himself; when, of course, he soon discovers that poor Mr. Spurrell is as much deceived as anybody else. What is he to do? Humiliate the unfortunate man by letting him know the truth? Mortify my uncle and aunt by a public explanation before a whole dinner-party? That is what a stupid or a selfish man might have done, almost without thinking. But not Mr. Blair. He has too much tact, too much imagination, too much chivalry for that. He saw at once that his only course was to spare his host and hostess, and—and all of us a scene, by slipping away quietly and unostentatiously, as he had come.

LADY RHONDA - (yawning). If he saw all that, why didn't he do it?

LADY MAISIE - (indignantly). Why? How provoking you can be, Rhoda! Why? Because that stupid Tredwell wouldn't let him! Because Archie delayed him by some idiotic practical joke! Because Mr. Spurrell went and blurted it all out!... Oh, don't try to run down a really fine act like that; because you can't—you simply can't!

LADY RHONDA - (after a low whistle). No idea it had gone so far as that—already! Now I begin to see why Gerry Thicknesse has been lookin' as if he'd sat on his best hat, and why he told your aunt he might have to be off to-morrow; which is all stuff, because I happen to know his leave ain't up for two or three days yet. But he sees this Troubadour has put his poor old nose out of joint for him.

LADY MAISIE - (flushing). Now, Rhoda, I won't have you talking as if—as if— You ought to know, if Gerald Thicknesse doesn't, that it's nothing at all of that sort! It's just— Oh, I can't tell you how some of his poems moved me, what new ideas, wider views they seemed to teach; and then how dreadfully it hurt to think it was only Mr. Spurrell after all!... But now—oh, the relief of finding they're not spoilt; that I can still admire, still look up to the man who wrote them! Not to have to feel that he is quite commonplace—not even a gentleman—in the ordinary sense!

LADY RHONDA - (rising). Ah well, I prefer a hero who looks as if he had his hair cut, occasionally—but then, I'm not romantic. He may be the paragon you say; but if I was you, my dear, I wouldn't expect too much of that young man—allow a margin for shrinkage, don't you know. And now I think I'll turn into my little crib, for I'm dead tired. Good night; don't sit up late readin' poetry; it's my opinion you've read quite enough as it is!

[She goes.

LADY MAISIE - (alone, as she gazes dreamily into the fire). She doesn't in the least understand! She actually suspects me of— As if I could possibly—or as if mamma would ever—even if he— Oh, how silly I am!... I don't care! I am glad I haven't had to give up my ideal. I should like to know him better. What harm is there in that? And if Gerald chooses to go to-morrow, he must—that's all. He isn't nearly so nice as he used to be; and he has even less imagination than ever! I don't think I could care for anybody so absolutely matter-of-fact. And yet, only an hour ago I almost— But that was before!


PART XXI

THE FEELINGS OF A MOTHER.

In the Morning Room.

TIME—Sunday morning; just after breakfast.

CAPTAIN THICKNESSE - (outside, to TREDWELL). Dogcart round, eh? everything in? All right—shan't be a minute. (Entering.) Hallo, Pilliner, you all alone here? (He looks round disconcertedly.) Don't happen to have seen Lady Maisie about?

PILLINER - Let me see—she was here a little while ago, I fancy.... Why? Do you want her?

CAPTAIN THICKNESSE - No—only to say good-bye and that. I'm just off.

PILLINER - Off? To-day! You don't mean to tell me your chief is such an inconsiderate old ruffian as to expect you to travel back to your Tommies on the Sabbath! You could wait till to-morrow if you wanted to. Come now!

CAPTAIN THICKNESSE - Perhaps—only, you see, I don't want to.

PILLINER - Well, tastes differ. I shouldn't call a cross-country journey in a slow train, with unlimited opportunities of studying the company's bye-laws and traffic arrangements at several admirably ventilated junctions, the ideal method of spending a cheery Sunday, myself, that's all.

CAPTAIN THICKNESSE - (gloomily). Dare say it will be about as cheery as stoppin' on here, if it comes to that.

PILLINER - I admit we were most of us a wee bit chippy at breakfast. The bard conversed—I will say that for him—but he seemed to diffuse a gloom somehow. Shut you up once or twice in a manner that might almost be described as damned offensive.

CAPTAIN THICKNESSE - Don't know what you all saw in what he said that was so amusin'. Confounded rude I thought it!

PILLINER - Don't think anyone was amused—unless it was LADY MAISIE - By the way, he might perhaps have selected a happier topic to hold forth to Sir Rupert on than the scandalous indifference of large landowners to the condition of the rural labourer. Poor dear old boy, he stood it wonderfully, considering. Pity Lady Cantire breakfasted upstairs; she'd have enjoyed herself. However, he had a very good audience in little Lady Maisie.

CAPTAIN THICKNESSE - I do hate a chap that jaws at breakfast.... Where did you say she was?

LADY MAISIE'S VOICE - (outside, in conservatory). Yes, you really ought to see the orangery and the Elizabethan garden, Mr. Blair. If you will be on the terrace in about five minutes, I could take you round myself. I must go and see if I can get the keys first.

PILLINER - If you want to say good-bye, old fellow, now's your chance!

CAPTAIN THICKNESSE - It—it don't matter. She's engaged. And, look here, you needn't mention that I was askin' for her.

PILLINER - Of course, old fellow, if you'd rather not. (He glances at him.) But I say, my dear old chap, if that's how it is with you, I don't quite see the sense of chucking it up already, don't you know. No earthly affair of mine, I know; still, if I could manage to stay on, I would, if I were you.

CAPTAIN THICKNESSE - Hang it all, Pilliner, do you suppose I don't know when the game's up! If it was any good stayin' on— And besides, I've said good-bye to Lady C., and all that. No, it's too late now.

TREDWELL - (at the door). Excuse me, sir, but if you're going by the 10.40, you haven't any too much time.

PILLINER - (to himself after CAPTAIN THICKNESSE has hurried out). Poor old chap, he does seem hard hit! Pity he's not Lady Maisie's sort. Though what she can see in that long-haired beggar—! Wonder when Vivien Spelwane intends to come down; never knew her miss breakfast before.... What's that rustling?... Women! I'll be off, or they'll nail me for church before I know it.

[He disappears hastily in the direction of the Smoking-room as LADY CANTIRE and MRS CHATTERIS enter.

LADY CANTIRE - Nonsense, my dear, no walk at all; the church is only just across the park. My brother Rupert always goes, and it pleases him to see the Wyvern pew as full as possible. I seldom feel equal to going myself, because I find the necessity of allowing pulpit inaccuracies to pass without a protest gets too much on my nerves; but my daughter will accompany you. You'll have just time to run up and get your things on.

MRS CHATTERIS - (with arch significance). I don't fancy I shall have the pleasure of your daughter's society this morning. I just met her going to get the garden keys; I think she has promised to show the grounds to— Well, I needn't mention whom. Oh dear me, I hope I'm not being indiscreet again!

LADY CANTIRE - I make a point of never interfering with my daughter's proceedings, and you can easily understand how natural it is that such old friends as they have always been—

MRS CHATTERIS - Really? I thought they seemed to take a great pleasure in one another's society. It's quite romantic. But I must rush up and get my bonnet on if I'm to go to church. (To herself, as she goes out.) So she was "Lady Grisoline," after all! If I was her mother— But dear Lady Cantire is so advanced about things.

LADY CANTIRE - (to herself). Darling Maisie! He'll be Lord Dunderhead before very long. How sensible and sweet of her! And I was quite uneasy about them last night at dinner; they scarcely seemed to be talking to each other at all. But there's a great deal more in dear Maisie than one would imagine.

SIR RUPERT CULVERIN - (outside). We're rather proud of our church, Mr. Undershell—fine old monuments and brasses, if you care about that sort of thing. Some of us will be walking over to service presently, if you would like to—

UNDERSHELL - (outside—to himself). And lose my tête-à-tête with Lady Maisie! Not exactly! (Aloud.) I am afraid, Sir Rupert, that I cannot conscientiously—

SIR RUPERT CULVERIN - (hastily). Oh, very well, very well; do exactly as you like about it, of course. I only thought— (To himself.) Now, that other young chap would have gone!

LADY CANTIRE - Rupert, who is that you are talking to out there? I don't recognise his voice, somehow.

SIR RUPERT CULVERIN - (entering with UNDERSHELL). Ha, Rohesia, you've come down, then? slept well, I hope. I was talking to a gentleman whose acquaintance I know you will be very happy to make—at last. This is the genuine celebrity this time. (To UNDERSHELL.) Let me make you known to my sister, Lady Cantire, Mr. UNDERSHELL - (As LADY CANTIRE glares interrogatively.) Mr. Clarion Blair, Rohesia, author of hum—ha—Andromache.

LADY CANTIRE - I thought we were given to understand last night that Mr. Spurrell—Mr. Blair—you must pardon me, but it's really so very confusing—that the writer of the—ah—volume in question had already left Wyvern.

SIR RUPERT CULVERIN - Well, my dear, you see he is still here—er—fortunately for us. If you'll excuse me, I'll leave Mr. Blair to entertain you; got to speak to Adams about something.

[He hurries out.

UNDERSHELL - (to himself). This must be Lady Maisie's mamma. Better be civil to her, I suppose; but I can't stay here and entertain her long! (Aloud.) Lady Cantire, I—er—have an appointment for which I am already a little late; but before I go, I should like to tell you how much pleasure it has given me to know that my poor verse has won your approval; appreciation from—

LADY CANTIRE - I'm afraid you must have been misinformed, Mr.—a—Blair. There are so many serious publications claiming attention in these days of literary over-production that I have long made it a rule to read no literature of a lighter order that has not been before the world for at least ten years. I may be mistaken, but I infer from your appearance that your own work must be of a considerably more recent date.

UNDERSHELL - (to himself). If she imagines she's going to snub Me—! (Aloud.) Then I was evidently mistaken in gathering from some expressions in your daughter's letter that—

LADY CANTIRE - Entirely. You are probably thinking of some totally different person, as my daughter has never mentioned having written to you, and is not in the habit of conducting any correspondence without my full knowledge and approval. I think you said you had some appointment; if so, pray don't consider yourself under any necessity to remain here.

UNDERSHELL - You are very good; I will not. (To himself, as he retires.) Awful old lady, that! I quite thought she would know all about that letter, or I should never have— However, I said nothing to compromise any one, luckily!

LADY CULERIN - (entering). Good morning, Rohesia. So glad you felt equal to coming down. I was almost afraid—after last night, you know.

LADY CANTIRE - (offering a cold cheekbone for salutation). I am in my usual health, thank you, Albinia. As to last night, if you must ask a literary Socialist down here, you might at least see that he is received with common courtesy. You may, for anything you can tell, have advanced the Social Revolution ten years in a single evening!

LADY CULVERIN - My dear Rohesia! If you remember, it was you yourself who—!

LADY CANTIRE - (closing her eyes). I am in no condition to argue about it, Albinia. The slightest exercise of your own common sense would have shown you— But there, no great harm has been done, fortunately, so let us say no more about it. I have something more agreeable to talk about. I've every reason to hope that Maisie and dear Gerald Thicknesse—

LADY CULERIN - (astonished). Maisie? But I thought Gerald Thicknesse spoke as if—!

LADY CANTIRE - Very possibly, my dear. I have always refrained from giving him the slightest encouragement, and I wouldn't put any pressure upon dear Maisie for the world—still, I have my feelings as a mother, and I can't deny that, with such prospects as he has now, it is gratifying for me to think that they may be coming to an understanding together at this very moment. She is showing him the grounds; which I always think are the great charm of Wyvern, so secluded!

LADY CULERIN - (puzzled). Together! At this very moment! But—but surely Gerald has gone?

LADY CANTIRE - Gone! What nonsense, Albinia! Where in the world should he have gone to?

LADY CULVERIN - He was leaving by the 10.40, I know. For Aldershot. I ordered the cart for him, and he said good-bye after breakfast. He seemed so dreadfully down, poor fellow, and I quite concluded from what he said that Maisie must have—

LADY CANTIRE - Impossible, my dear, quite impossible! I tell you he is here. Why, only a few minutes ago, Mrs. Chatteris was telling me— Ah, here she is to speak for herself. (To Mrs. Chatteris, who appears, arrayed for divine service.) Mrs. Chatteris, did I, or did I not, understand you to say just now that my daughter Maisie—?

MRS CHATTERIS - (alarmed). But, dear Lady Cantire, I had no idea you would disapprove. Indeed you seemed— And really, though she certainly seems to find him rather well—sympathetic—I'm sure— almost sure—there can be nothing serious—at present.

LADY CANTIRE - Thank you, my dear, I merely wished for an answer to my question. And you see, Albinia, that Gerald Thicknesse can hardly have gone yet, since he is walking about the grounds with Maisie.

Mrs. Chatteris. Captain Thicknesse? But he has gone, Lady Cantire! I saw him start. I didn't mean him.

LADY CANTIRE - Indeed? then I shall be obliged if you will say who it is you did mean.

Mrs. Chatteris. Why, only her old friend and admirer—that little poet man, Mr. Blair.

LADY CANTIRE - (to herself). And I actually sent him to her! (Rising in majestic wrath.) Albinia, whatever comes of this, remember I shall hold you entirely responsible!

[She sweeps out of the room; the other two ladies look after her, and then at one another, in silent consternation.


PART XXII

A DESCENT FROM THE CLOUDS

In the Elizabethan Garden. Lady MAISIE and UNDERSHELL are on a seat in the Yew Walk.

TIME—About 11 A.M.

LADY MAISIE - (softly). And you really meant to go away, and never let one of us know what had happened to you!

UNDERSHELL - (to himself). How easy it is after all to be a hero! (Aloud.) That certainly was my intention, only I was—er—not permitted to carry it out. I trust you don't consider I should have been to blame?

LADY MAISIE - (with shining eyes). To blame? Mr. Blair! As if I could possibly do that! (To herself.) He doesn't even see how splendid it was of him!

UNDERSHELL - (to himself). I begin to believe that I can do no wrong in her eyes! (Aloud.) It was not altogether easy, believe me, to leave without even having seen your face; but I felt so strongly that it was better so.

LADY MAISIE - (looking down). And—do you still feel that?

UNDERSHELL - I must confess that I am well content to have failed. It was such unspeakable torture to think that you, Lady Maisie, you of all people, would derive your sole idea of my personality from such an irredeemable vulgarian as that veterinary surgeon—the man Spurrell!

LADY MAISIE - (to herself, with an almost imperceptible start). I suppose it's only natural he should feel like that—but I wish—I do wish he had put it just a little differently! (Aloud.) Poor Mr. Spurrell! perhaps he was not exactly—

UNDERSHELL - Not exactly! I assure you it is simply inconceivable to me that, in a circle of any pretensions to culture and refinement, an ill-bred boor like that could have been accepted for a single moment as—I won't say a Man of Genius, but—

LADY MAISIE - (the light dying out of her eyes). No, don't—don't go on, Mr. Blair. We were all excessively stupid, no doubt, but you must make allowances for us—for me, especially. I have had so few opportunities of meeting people who are really distinguished—in literature, at least. Most of the people I know best are—well, not exactly clever, you know. I so often wish I was in a set that cared rather more about intellectual things!

UNDERSHELL - (with infinite pity). How you must have pined for freer air! How you must have starved on such mental provender as, for example, the vapid and inane commonplaces of that swaggering carpet-soldier, Captain—Thickset, isn't it?

LADY MAISIE - (drawing back into her corner). You evidently don't know that CAPTAIN THICKNESSE distinguished himself greatly in the Soudan, where he was very severely wounded.

UNDERSHELL - Possibly; but that is scarcely to the point. I do not question his efficiency as a fighting animal. As to his intelligence, perhaps, the less said the better.

LADY MAISIE - (contracting her brows). Decidedly. I ought to have mentioned at once that Captain Thicknesse is a very old friend of mine.

UNDERSHELL - Really? He, at least, may be congratulated. But pray don't think that I spoke with any personal animus; I merely happen to entertain a peculiar aversion for a class whose profession is systematic slaughter. In these Democratic times, when Humanity is advancing by leaps and bounds towards International Solidarity, soldiers are such grotesque and unnecessary anachronisms.

LADY MAISIE - (to herself, with a little shiver). Oh, why does he—why does he? (Aloud.) I should have thought that, until war itself is an anachronism, men who are willing to fight and die for their country could never be quite unnecessary. But we won't discuss Captain Thicknesse, particularly now that he has left Wyvern. Suppose we go back to Mr. SPURRELL - I know, of course, that, in leaving him in ignorance as you did, you acted from the best and highest motives; but still—

UNDERSHELL - It is refreshing to be so thoroughly understood! I think I know what your "but still" implies—why did I not foresee that he would infallibly betray himself before long? I did. But I gave him credit for being able to sustain his part for another hour or two—until I had gone, in fact.

LADY MAISIE - Then you didn't wish to spare his feelings as well as ours?

UNDERSHELL - To be quite frank, I didn't trouble myself about him: my sole object was to retreat with dignity; he had got himself somehow or other into a false position he must get out of as best he could. After all, he would be none the worse for having filled my place for a few hours.

LADY MAISIE - (slowly). I see. It didn't matter to you whether he was suspected of being an impostor, or made to feel uncomfortable, or—or anything. Wasn't that a little unfeeling of you?

UNDERSHELL - Unfeeling! I allowed him to keep my evening clothes, which is more than a good many—

LADY MAISIE - At all events, he may have had to pay more heavily than you imagine. I wonder whether— But I suppose anything so unromantic as the love affairs of a veterinary surgeon would have no interest for you?

UNDERSHELL - Why not, Lady Maisie? To the Student of Humanity, and still more to the Poet, the humblest love-story may have its interesting—even its suggestive—aspect.

LADY MAISIE - Well, I may tell you that it seems Mr. Spurrell has long been attached, if not actually engaged, to a maid of mine.

UNDERSHELL - (startled out of his self-possession). You—you don't mean to Miss Phillipson?

LADY MAISIE - That is her name. How very odd that you— But perhaps Mr. Spurrell mentioned it to you last night?

UNDERSHELL - (recovering his sangfroid). I am hardly likely to have heard of it from any other quarter.

LADY MAISIE - Of course not. And did he tell you that she was here, in this very house?

UNDERSHELL - No, he never mentioned that. What a remarkable coincidence!

LADY MAISIE - Yes, rather. The worst of it is that the foolish girl seems to have heard that he was a guest here, and have jumped to the conclusion that he had ceased to care for her; so she revenged herself by a desperate flirtation with some worthless wretch she met in the housekeeper's room, whose flattery and admiration, I'm very much afraid, have completely turned her head!

UNDERSHELL - (uncomfortably). Ah, well, she must learn to forget him, and no doubt, in time— How wonderful the pale sunlight is on that yew hedge!

LADY MAISIE - You are not very sympathetic! I should not have told you at all, only I wanted to show you that if poor Mr. Spurrell did innocently usurp your place, he may have lost— But I see all this only bores you.

UNDERSHELL - Candidly, Lady Maisie, I can't affect a very keen interest in the—er—gossip of the housekeeper's room. Indeed, I am rather surprised that you should condescend to listen to—

LADY MAISIE - (to herself). This is really too much! (Aloud.) It never occurred to me that I was "condescending" in taking an interest in a pretty and wayward girl who happens to be my maid. But then, I'm not a Democrat, Mr. Blair.

UNDERSHELL - I—I'm afraid you construed my remark as a rebuke; which it was not at all intended to be.

LADY MAISIE - It would have been rather superfluous if it had been, wouldn't it? (Observing his growing uneasiness.) I'm afraid you don't find this bench quite comfortable?

UNDERSHELL - I—er—moderately so. (To himself.) There's a female figure coming down the terrace steps. It's horribly like— But that must be my morbid fancy; still, if I can get Lady Maisie away, just in case— (Aloud.) D—don't you think sitting still becomes a little—er—monotonous after a time? Couldn't we—

[He rises, spasmodically.

LADY MAISIE - (rising too). Certainly; we have sat here quite long enough. It is time we went back.

UNDERSHELL - (to himself). We shall meet her! and I'm almost sure it's— I must prevent any— (Aloud.) Not back, Lady Maisie! You—you promised to show me the orchid-house—you did, indeed!

LADY MAISIE - Very well; we can go in, if you care about orchids. It's on our way back.

UNDERSHELL - (to himself). This is too awful! It is that girl Phillipspn. She is looking for somebody! Me! (Aloud.) On second thoughts, I don't think I do care to see the orchids. I detest them; they are such weird, unnatural, extravagant things. Let us turn back and see if there are any snowdrops on the lawn behind that hedge. I love the snowdrop, it is so trustful and innocent, with its pure green-veined— Do come and search for snowdrops!

LADY MAISIE - Not just now. I think—(as she shields her eyes with one hand)—I'm not quite sure yet— but I rather fancy that must be my maid at the other end of the walk.

UNDERSHELL - (eagerly). I assure you, Lady Maisie, you are quite mistaken. Not the least like her!

LADY MAISIE - (astonished). Why, how can you possibly tell that, without having seen her, Mr. Blair?

UNDERSHELL - I—I meant— You described her as "pretty," you know. This girl is plain—distinctly plain!

LADY MAISIE - I don't agree at all. However, it certainly is Phillipson, and she seems to have come out in search of me; so I had better see if she has any message.

UNDERSHELL - She hasn't. I'm positive she hasn't. She—she wouldn't walk like that if she had. (In feverish anxiety.) Lady Maisie, shall we turn back? She—she hasn't seen us yet!

LADY MAISIE - Really, Mr. Blair! I don't quite see why I should run away from my own maid!... What is it, Phillipson?

[She advances to meet PHILLIPSON, leaving UNDERSHELL behind, motionless.

UNDERSHELL - (to himself). It's all over! That confounded girl recognises me. I saw her face change! She'll be jealous, I know she'll be jealous—and then she'll tell Lady Maisie everything!... I wish to Heaven I could hear what she is saying. Lady Maisie seems agitated.... I—I might stroll gently on and leave them; but it would look too like running away, perhaps. No, I'll stay here and face it out like a man! I won't give up just yet. (He sinks limply upon the bench.) After all, I've been in worse holes than this since I came into this infernal place, and I've always managed to scramble out—triumphantly too! If she will only give me five minutes alone, I know I can clear myself; it isn't as if I had done anything to be ashamed of.... She's sent away that girl. She seems to be expecting me to come to her.... I—I suppose I'd better.

[He rises with effort, and goes towards Lady MAISIE with a jaunty unconsciousness that somehow has the air of stopping short just above the knees.


PART XXIII

SHRINKAGE

In the Yew Walk.

LADY MAISIE - (to herself, as she watches UNDERSHELL approaching). How badly he walks, and what does he mean by smiling at me like that? (Aloud, coldly.) I am sorry, Mr. Blair, but I must leave you to finish your stroll alone; my maid has just told me—

UNDERSHELL - (vehemently). Lady Maisie, I ask you, in common fairness, not to judge me until you have heard my version. You will not allow the fact that I travelled down here in the same compartment with your maid, Phillipson—

LADY MAISIE - (wide-eyed). The same! But we came by that train. I thought you missed it?

UNDERSHELL - I—I was not so fortunate. It is rather a long and complicated story, but—

LADY MAISIE - I'm afraid I really can't listen to you now, Mr. Blair, after what I have heard from Phillipson—

UNDERSHELL - I implore you not to go without hearing both sides. Sit down again—if only for a minute. I feel confident that I can explain everything satisfactorily.

LADY MAISIE - (sitting down). I can't imagine what there is to explain—and really I ought, if Phillipson—

UNDERSHELL - You know what maids are, Lady Maisie. They embroider. Unintentionally, I dare say, but still, they do embroider.

LADY MAISIE - (puzzled). She is very clever at mending lace, I know, though what that has to do with it—

UNDERSHELL - Listen to me, Lady Maisie. I came to this house at your bidding. Yes, but for your written appeal, I should have treated the invitation I received from your aunt with silent contempt. Had I obeyed my first impulse and ignored it, I should have been spared humiliations and indignities which ought rather to excite your pity than—than any other sensation. Think—try to realise what my feelings must have been when I found myself expected by the butler here to sit down to supper with him and the upper servants in the housekeeper's room!

LADY MAISIE - (shocked). Oh, Mr. Blair! Indeed, I had no—You weren't really! How could they? What did you say?

UNDERSHELL - (haughtily). I believe I let him know my opinion of the snobbery of his employers in treating a guest of theirs so cavalierly.

LADY MAISIE - (distressed). But surely—surely you couldn't suppose that my uncle and aunt were capable of—

UNDERSHELL - What else could I suppose, under the circumstances? It is true I have since learnt that I was mistaken in this particular instance; but I am not ignorant of the ingrained contempt you aristocrats have for all who live by exercising their intellect—the bitter scorn of birth for brains!

LADY MAISIE - I am afraid the—the contempt is all on the other side; but if that is how you feel about it, I don't wonder that you were indignant.

UNDERSHELL - Indignant! I was furious. In fact, nothing would have induced me to sit down to supper at all, if it hadn't been for—

LADY MAISIE - (in a small voice). Then—you did sit down? With the servants! Oh, Mr. Blair!

UNDERSHELL - I thought you were already aware of it. Yes, Lady Maisie, I endured even that. But (with magnanimity) you must not distress yourself about it now. If I can forget it, surely you can do so!

LADY MAISIE - Can I? That you should have consented, for any consideration whatever; how could you—how could you?

UNDERSHELL - (to himself). She admires me all the more for it. But I knew she would take the right view! (Aloud, with pathos.) I was only compelled by absolute starvation. I had had an unusually light lunch, and I was so hungry!

LADY MAISIE - (after a pause). That explains it, of course.... I hope they gave you a good supper!

UNDERSHELL - Excellent, thank you. Indeed, I was astonished at the variety and even luxury of the table. There was a pyramid of quails—

LADY MAISIE - I am pleased to hear it. But I thought there was something you were going to explain.

UNDERSHELL - I have been endeavouring to explain to the best of my ability that if I have undesignedly been the cause of—er—a temporary diversion in the state of Miss Phillipson's affections, no one could regret more deeply than I that the—er—ordinary amenities of the supper-table should have been mistaken for—

LADY MAISIE - (horrified). Oh, stop, Mr. Blair, please stop! I don't want to hear any more. I see now. It was you who—

UNDERSHELL - Of course it was I. Surely the girl herself has been telling you so just now!

LADY MAISIE - You really thought that possible, too? She simply came with a message from my mother.

UNDERSHELL - (slightly disconcerted). Oh! If I had known it was merely that. However, I am sure I need not ask you to treat my—my communication in the strictest confidence, Lady Maisie.

LADY MAISIE - Indeed, that is perfectly unnecessary, Mr. Blair.

UNDERSHELL - Yes, I felt from the first that I could trust you—even with my life. And I cannot regret having told you, if it has enabled you to understand me more thoroughly. It is such a relief that you know all, and that there are no more secrets between us. You do feel that I only acted as was natural and inevitable under the circumstances?

LADY MAISIE - Oh yes, yes. I—I dare say you could not help it. I mean you did quite, quite right!

UNDERSHELL - Ah, how you comfort me with your fresh girlish— You are not going, Lady Maisie?

LADY MAISIE - (rising). I must. I ought to have gone before. My mother wants me. No, you are not to come too; you can go on and gather those snowdrops, you know.

[She walks slowly back to the house.

UNDERSHELL - (looking after her). She took it wonderfully well. I've made it all right, or she wouldn't have said that about the snowdrops. Yes, she shall not be disappointed; she shall have her posy!

In the Morning-room. Half an hour later.

LADY MAISIE - (alone—to herself). Thank goodness, that's over! It was awful. I don't think I ever saw mamma a deeper shade of plum colour! How I have been mistaken in Mr. Blair! That he could write those lines—

"Aspiring unto that far-off Ideal,
I may not stoop to any meaner love,"

—and yet philander with my poor foolish Phillipson the moment he met her! And then to tell mamma about my letter like that! Why, even Mr. Spurrell had more discretion—to be sure, he knew nothing about it—but that makes no difference! Rhoda was right; I ought to have allowed a margin—only I should never have allowed margin enough! The worst of it is that, if mamma was unjust in some things she said, she was right about one. I have disgusted Gerald. He mayn't be brilliant, but at least he's straightforward and loyal and a gentleman, and—and he did like me once. He doesn't any more—or he wouldn't have gone away. And it may be ages before I ever get a chance to let him see how dreadfully sorry— (She turns, and sees Captain THICKNESSE.) Oh, haven't you gone yet?

CAPTAIN THICKNESSE - Yes, I went, but I've come back again. I—I couldn't help it; 'pon my word I couldn't.

LADY MAISIE - (with a sudden flush) You—you weren't sent for—by—by any one?

CAPTAIN THICKNESSE - So likely any one would send for me, isn't it?

LADY MAISIE - I don't know why I said that; it was silly, of course. But how—

CAPTAIN THICKNESSE - Ran it a bit too fine; got to Shuntin'bridge just in time to see the tail end of the train disappearin'; wasn't another for hours—not much to do there, don't you know.

LADY MAISIE - You might have taken a walk—or gone to church.

CAPTAIN THICKNESSE - So I might, didn't occur to me; and besides, I—I remembered I never said good-bye to you.

LADY MAISIE - Didn't you? And whose fault was that?

CAPTAIN THICKNESSE - Not mine, anyhow. You were somewhere about the grounds with Mr. Blair.

LADY MAISIE - Now you mention it, I believe I was. We had—rather an interesting conversation. Still, you might have come to look for me!

CAPTAIN THICKNESSE - Perhaps you wouldn't have been over and above glad to see me.

LADY MAISIE - Oh yes, I should!—When it was to say good-bye, you know!

CAPTAIN THICKNESSE - Ah! Well, I suppose I shall only be in the way if I stop here any longer now.

LADY MAISIE - Do you? What makes you suppose that?

CAPTAIN THICKNESSE - Nothin'! Saw your friend the bard hurryin' along the terrace with a bunch of snowdrops; he'll be here in another—

LADY MAISIE - (in unmistakable horror). Gerald, why didn't you tell me before? There's only just time!

[She flies to a door and opens it.

CAPTAIN THICKNESSE - But I say, you know! Maisie, may I come too?

LADY MAISIE - Don't be a goose, Gerald. Of course you can, if you like.

[She disappears in the conservatory.

CAPTAIN THICKNESSE - (to himself). Can't quite make this out, but I'm no end glad I came back!

[He follows quickly.

UNDERSHELL - (entering). I hoped I should find her here. (He looks round.) Her mother's gone—that's something! I dare say Lady Maisie will come in presently. (He sits down and re-arranges his snowdrops.) It will be sweet to see her face light up when I offer her these as a symbol of the new and closer link between us! (He hears the sound of drapery behind him.) Ah, already! (Rising, and presenting his flowers with downcast eyes.) I—I have ventured to gather these—for you. (He raises his eyes.) Miss Spelwane!

MISS SPELWANE - (taking them graciously). How very sweet of you, Mr. Blair. Are they really for me?

UNDERSHELL - (concealing his disappointment). Oh—er—yes. If you will give me the pleasure of accepting them.

MISS SPELWANE - I feel immensely proud. I was so afraid you must have thought I was rather cross to you last night. I didn't mean to be. I was feeling a little overdone, that was all. But you have chosen a charming way of letting me see that I am forgiven. (To herself.) It's really too touching. He certainly is a great improvement on the other wretch!

UNDERSHELL - (dolefully). I—I had no such intention, I assure you. (To himself.) I hope to goodness Lady Maisie won't come in before I can get rid of this girl. I seem fated to be misunderstood here!


PART XXIV

THE HAPPY DISPATCH

"Perhaps it was right to dissemble your love, but—"

In the Morning-room.

TIME—About 1 P.M.

UNDERSHELL - (to himself alone). I'm rather sorry that that Miss Spelwane couldn't stay. She's a trifle angular—but clever. It was distinctly sharp of her to see through that fellow Spurrell from the first, and lay such an ingenious little trap for him. And she has a great feeling for Literature—knows my verses by heart, I discovered, quite accidentally. All the same, I wish she hadn't intercepted those snowdrops. Now I shall have to go out and pick some more. (Sounds outside in the entrance hall.) Too late—they've got back from church!

MRS BROOKE-CHATTERIS - (entering with LADY RHONDA, SIR RUPERT and BEARPARK). Such a nice, plain, simple service—I'm positively ravenous!

LADY RHONDA - Struck me some of those chubby choir-boys wanted smackin'. What a business it seems to get the servants properly into their pew—as bad as boxin' a string of hunters! As for you, Archie, the way you fidgeted durin' the sermon was downright disgraceful!... So there you are, Mr. Blair; not been to church; but I forgot—p'raps you're a Dissenter, or somethin'?

UNDERSHELL - (annoyed). Only, Lady Rhonda, in the sense that I have hitherto failed to discover any form of creed that commands my intellectual assent.

LADY RHONDA - (unimpressed). I expect you haven't tried. Are you a—what d'ye call it?—a Lacedemoniac?

UNDERSHELL - (with lofty tolerance). I presume you mean a "Laodicean." No, I should rather describe myself as a Deist.

ARCHIE BEARPARK - (in a surly undertone). What's a Deast when he's at home? If he'd said a Beast, now! (Aloud, as PILLINER enters with CAPTAIN THICKNESSE.) Hullo, why, here's Thicknesse! So you haven't gone, after all, then?

CAPTAIN THICKNESSE - What an observant young beggar you are, Bearpark! Nothin' escapes you. No, I haven't. (To SIR RUPERT, rather sheepishly.) Fact, is, sir, I—I somehow just missed the train, and—and—thought I might as well come back, instead of waitin' about, don't you know.

SIR RUPERT CULVERIN - (heartily). Why, of course, my dear boy, of course! Never have forgiven you if you hadn't. Great nuisance for you, though. Hope you blew the fool of a man up; he ought to have been round in plenty of time.

CAPTAIN THICKNESSE - Not the groom's fault, sir. I kept him waitin' a bit, and—and we had to stop to shift the seat and that, and so—

UNDERSHELL - (to himself). Great blundering booby! Can't he see nobody wants him here? As if he hadn't bored poor Lady Maisie enough at breakfast! Ah, well, I must come to her rescue once more, I suppose!

SIR RUPERT CULVERIN - Half an hour to lunch! Anybody like to come round to the stables? I'm going to see how my wife's horse Deerfoot is getting on. Fond of horses, eh, Mr.—a—Undershell? Care to come with us?

UNDERSHELL - (to himself). I've seen quite enough of that beast already! (Aloud, with some asperity.) You must really excuse me, Sir. I am at one with Mr. Ruskin—I detest horses.

SIR RUPERT CULVERIN - Ah? Pity. We're rather fond of 'em here. But we can't expect a poet to be a sportsman, eh?

UNDERSHELL - For my own poor part, I confess I look forward to a day, not far distant, when the spread of civilisation will have abolished every form of so-called Sport.

SIR RUPERT CULVERIN - Do you, though? (After conquering a choke with difficulty.) Allow me to hope that you will continue to enjoy the pleasures of anticipation as long as possible. (To the rest.) Well, are you coming?

[All except UNDERSHELL follow their host out.

UNDERSHELL - (alone, to himself). If they think I'm going to be patronised, or suppress my honest convictions—! Now I'll go and pick those—(Lady MAISIE enters from the conservatory.) Ah, Lady Maisie, I have been trying to find you. I had plucked a few snowdrops, which I promised myself the pleasure of presenting to you. Unfortunately they—er—failed to reach their destination.

LADY MAISIE - (distantly). Thanks, Mr. Blair; I am only sorry you should have given yourself such unnecessary trouble.

UNDERSHELL - (detaining her, as she seemed about to pass on). I have another piece of intelligence which you may hear less—er—philosophically, LADY MAISIE - Your bête noire has returned.

LADY MAISIE - (with lifted eyebrows). My bête noire, Mr. Blair?

UNDERSHELL - Why affect not to understand? I have an infallible instinct in all matters concerning you, and, sweetly tolerant as you are, I instantly divined what an insufferable nuisance you found our military friend, Captain Thicknesse.

LADY MAISIE - There are limits even to my tolerance, Mr. Blair. I admit I find some people insufferable—but Captain Thicknesse is not one of them.

UNDERSHELL - Then appearances are deceptive indeed. Come, Lady Maisie, surely you can trust me!

[LADY CANTIRE enters.

LADY CANTIRE - (in her most awful tones). Maisie, my dear, I appear to have interrupted an interview of a somewhat confidential character. If so, pray let me know it, and I will go elsewhere.

LADY MAISIE - (calmly). Not in the very least, mamma. Mr. Blair was merely trying to prepare me for the fact that Captain Thicknesse has come back; which was quite needless, as I happen to have heard it already from his own lips.

LADY CANTIRE – Captain Thicknesse come back! (To UNDERSHELL.) I wish to speak to my daughter. May I ask you to leave us?

UNDERSHELL - With pleasure, Lady Cantire. (To himself, as he retires.) What a consummate actress that girl is! And what a coquette!

LADY CANTIRE - (after a silence). Maisie, what does all this mean? No nonsense, now! What brought Gerald Thicknesse back?

LADY MAISIE - I suppose the dog-cart, mamma. He missed his train, you know. I don't think he minds—much.

LADY CANTIRE - Let me tell you this, my dear. It is a great deal more than you deserve after—How long has he come back for?

LADY MAISIE - Only a few hours; but—but from things he said, I fancy he would stay on longer—if Aunt Albinia asked him.

LADY CANTIRE - Then we may consider that settled; he stays. (LADY CULVERIN appears.) Here is your aunt. You had better leave us, my dear.

Somewhat later; the Party have assembled for Lunch.

SIR RUPERT CULVERIN - (to his wife). Well, my dear, I've seen that young SPURRELL - (smart fellow he is, too, thoroughly up in his business), and you'll be glad to hear he can't find anything seriously wrong with Deerfoot.

UNDERSHELL - (in the background, to himself). No more could I, for that matter!

SIR RUPERT CULVERIN - He's clear it isn't navicular, which Adams was afraid of, and he thinks, with care and rest, you know, the horse will be as fit as a fiddle in a very few days.

UNDERSHELL - (to himself). Just exactly what I told them; but the fools wouldn't believe me!

LADY CULVERIN - Oh, Rupert, I am so glad. How clever of that nice Mr. Spurrell! I was afraid my poor Deerfoot would have to be shot.

UNDERSHELL - (to himself). She may thank me that he wasn't. And this other fellow gets all the credit for it. How like Life!

LADY MAISIE - And, Uncle Rupert, how about—about Phillipson, you know? Is it all right?

SIR RUPERT CULVERIN - Phillipson? Oh, why, 'pon my word, my dear, didn't think of asking.

LADY RHONDA - But I did, Maisie. And they met this mornin', and it's all settled, and they're as happy as they can be. Except that he's on the look out for a mysterious stranger, who disappeared last night, after tryin' to make desperate love to her. He is determined, if he can find him, to give him a piece of his mind.

[UNDERSHELL endeavours to conceal his extreme uneasiness.

PILLINER - And the whole of a horsewhip. He invited my opinion of it as an implement of castigation. Kind of thing, you know, that would impart "proficiency in the trois temps, as danced in the most select circles," in a single lesson to a lame bear. (To himself.) I drew my little bow at a venture, and I'm hanged if it hasn't touched him up! There's something fishy about this chap—I felt it all along. Still, I don't see what more I can do—or I'd do it, for poor old Gerry Thicknesse's sake.

UNDERSHELL - (to himself). I don't stir a step out of this house while I'm here, that's all!

SIR RUPERT CULVERIN - Ha-ha! Athletic young chap that. Glad to see him in the field next Tuesday. By the way, Albinia, you've heard how Thicknesse here contrived to miss his train this morning? Our gain, of course; but still we must manage to get you back to Aldershot to-night, my boy, or you'll get called over the coals by your colonel when you do put in an appearance, hey? Now, let's see; what train ought you to catch?

[He takes up "Bradshaw" from a writing-table.

LADY CANTIRE - (possessing herself of the volume). Allow me, Rupert, my eyes are better than yours. I will look out his trains for him. (After consulting various pages.) Just as I thought! Quite impossible for him to reach North Camp to-night now. There isn't a train till six, and that gets to town just too late for him to drive across to Waterloo and catch the last Aldershot train. So there's no more to be said.

[She puts "Bradshaw" away.

CAPTAIN THICKNESSE - (with undisguised relief). Oh, well, dessay they won't kick up much of a row if I don't get back till to-morrow,—or the day after, if it comes to that.

UNDERSHELL - (to himself). It shan't come to that—if I can prevent it! Lady Maisie is quite in despair, I can see. (Aloud.) Indeed? I was—a—not aware that discipline was quite so lax as that in the British Army. And surely officers should set an example of—

[He finds that his intervention has produced a distinct sensation, and, taking up the discarded "Bradshaw" becomes engrossed in its study.

CAPTAIN THICKNESSE - (ignoring him completely). It's like this, Lady Culverin. Somehow I—I muddled up the dates, don't you know. Mean to say, got it into my head to-day was the 20th, instead of only the 18th. (Lamely.) That's how it was.

LADY CULVERIN - Delightful, my dear Gerald. Then we shall keep you here till Tuesday, of course!

UNDERSHELL - (looking up from "Bradshaw," impulsively). Lady Culverin, I see there's a very good train which leaves Shuntingbridge at 3.15 this afternoon, and gets—

[The rest regard him with unaffected surprise and disapproval.

LADY CANTIRE - (raising her glasses). Upon my word, Mr. Blair! If you will kindly leave Captain Thicknesse to make his own arrangements—!

LADY MAISIE - (interposing hastily). But, mamma, you must have misunderstood Mr. Blair! As if he would dream of—He was merely mentioning the train he wishes to go by himself. Weren't you, Mr. Blair?

UNDERSHELL - (blinking and gasping). I—eh? Just so, that—that was my intention, certainly. (To himself.) Does she at all realise what this will cost her?

LADY CULVERIN - My dear Mr. Blair, I—I'd no notion we were to lose you so soon; but if you're really quite sure you must go—

LADY CANTIRE - (sharply). Really, Albinia, we must give him credit for knowing his own mind. He tells you he is obliged to go!

LADY CULVERIN - Then of course we must let you do exactly as you please.

PILLINER - (to himself). Lady Maisie's a little brick! No notion she had it in her. No occasion to bother myself about the beggar now. "Let him alone and he'll go home, and carry his tail beneath him!"

[All except MISS SPELWANE breathe more freely; TREDWELL appears.

LADY CULVERIN - Oh, lunch, is it, Tredwell? Very well. By the bye, see that some one packs Mr. Undershell's things for him, and tell them to send the dog-cart round after lunch in time to catch the 3.15 from Shuntingbridge.

ARCHIE BEARPARK - (sotto voce, to PILLINER). We don't want any more missin' of trains, eh? I'll go round and see the cart properly balanced myself this time.

PILLINER - (in the same tone). No, dear boy, you're not to be trusted! I'll see that done, then the bard and his train will be alike in one respect—neither of 'em 'll be missed!

MISS SPELWANE - (to herself, piqued.) Going already! I wish I had never touched his ridiculous snowdrops!

LADY CULVERIN - Well, shall we go in to lunch, everybody?

[They move in irregular order towards the dining-hall.

UNDERSHELL - (in an undertone to LADY MAISIE, as they follow last). Lady Maisie, I—er—this is just a little unexpected. I confess I don't quite understand your precise motive in suggesting so—so hasty a departure.

LADY MAISIE - (without looking at him). Don't you, Mr. Blair? Perhaps—when you come to think over it all quietly—you will.

[She passes on, leaving him perplexed.

UNDERSHELL - (to himself). Shall I? I certainly can't say I do just— Why, yes, I do! That bully Spurrell with his horsewhip! She dreads an encounter between us—and I should much prefer to avoid it myself. Yes; that's it, of course. She is willing to sacrifice anything rather than endanger my personal safety! What unselfish angels some women are! Even that sneering fellow Drysdale will be impressed when I tell him this.... Yes, it's best that I should go—I see that now. I don't so much mind leaving. Without any false humility, I can hardly avoid seeing that, even in the short time I have been amongst these people, I have produced a decided impression. And there is at least one—perhaps two—who will miss me when I am gone.

[He goes into the Dining-hall, with restored complacency.

F. Anstey -- A Concise Bibliography

Vice Versa (1882)
The Black Poodle And Other Tales (1884)
The Giant's Robe (1884)
The Tinted Venus (1885)
A Fallen Idol (1886)
Burglar Bill And Other Pieces (1888)
The Pariah (1889)

Voces Populi (1890)
Tourmalin's Time Cheques (1891)
Mr. Punch's Model Music-Hall Songs And Dramas (1892)
The Talking Horse And Other Tales (1892)
The Travelling Companions (1892)
The Man From Blankley's And Other Sketches (1893)
Mr. Punch's Pocket Ibsen (1893)
Under the Rose (1894)
Lyre and Lancet (1895)
The Statement of Stella Maberly, Written By Herself (1896)
Baboo Jabberjee, B. A. (1897)
Puppets At Large (1897)
Love Among The Lions (1898)
Paleface And Redskin (1898)
The Brass Bottle (1900)
A Bayard From Bengal (1902)
Only Toys! (1903)
Salted Almonds (1906)
Winnie, An Everyday Story (1909)
In Brief Authority (1915)
Percy and Others (1915)
The Last Load (1925)
The Would-Be Gentleman (Adapted From Molière's Le Bourgeois gentilhomme) (1927)
The Imaginary Invalid (Adapted From Molière's Le Malade imaginaire) (1929)
Humour and Fantasy (1931)
A Long Retrospect (1936)

www.ingramcontent.com/pod-product-compliance
Lightning Source LLC
Chambersburg PA
CBHW071411170626
46811CB00003B/1352